Dr John Treherne is a Fellow of Downing College, Cambridge, and *The Trap* is his first novel. He has previously published two non-fiction studies of very different communities in the 1930s: *The Galapagos Affair* and *The Strange History of Bonnie and Clyde*.

By the same author

The Galapagos Affair
The Strange History of Bonnie and Clyde

JOHN TREHERNE

The Trap

TRIAD
GRAFTON BOOKS

LONDON GLASGOW
TORONTO SYDNEY AUCKLAND

Triad
Grafton Books
8 Grafton Street, London W1X 3LA

Published by Triad Grafton 1986

Triad Paperbacks Ltd is an imprint of
Chatto, Bodley Head & Jonathan Cape Ltd and
Grafton Books, A Division of the Collins Publishing Group

First published in Great Britain by
Jonathan Cape Ltd 1985

ISBN 0-586-06840-6

Printed and bound in Great Britain by
Collins, Glasgow

Set in Times

To Paul, Tony and Margaret

1

The day started badly and then got worse. I had been awake and fretful for an hour before a damp October dawn, contemplating the improbability of being fifty-three and the awful prospect of De Freville. Then there was the quarrel with Molly at breakfast and the drive in the rain-soaked Marina to find the College car-park full.

My ten o'clock lecture was delivered to thirteen dispirited survivors of the bright-eyed horde who had gathered on a sunny morning at the beginning of term. Prominent in the otherwise empty front row was De Freville, a tall lugubrious undergraduate from my own College whose hostile stare nullified my attempts to enliven the complexities of the Peasants' Revolt. I remembered again, still smarting from the memory of the last supervision class when he had smirked throughout my carefully prepared exposition on medieval land tenure, that I would have to face his over-developed critical faculties that afternoon. Even in the full flood of my lecture, there stirred in my mind the terrifying, recurring fantasy of a De Freville world of supercilious and hypercritical young men, all with grating adenoidal accents, dominating the Faculty Board of History, the House of Commons and the boards of many companies.

Coffee in the lecturers' room was a dismal occasion on which, successively, the topics of mortgage repayments, dry rot, the petrol consumption of lecturers' cars and the latest scandals in the Faculty of English were discussed with great seriousness and, with the exception of the latter topic, considerable scholarly attention to detail. However, College lunch (rehydrated asparagus soup and macabre trout with bloodshot eyes of glacé cherries) was enlivened by the company of Oakley, the up-and-coming biologist.

Oakley, a small, gingery man, knew of my amateur passion for natural history and I was flattered that he should talk to me on almost equal terms. Not that he was professionally concerned with such gorgeous creatures as stone curlews or redshanks. In fact, I knew more about these than he did, but we could talk away about estuaries, wading birds and breeding behaviour as a sort of antidote to College gossip. Oakley clearly found it odd that a historian should be so obsessed with ornithology. But, as I had told him, it had been a childhood interest, ever since I had known a colourful rustic sponger, the local poacher, who had inadvertently sown the seeds of my passion for natural history. I had felt a twinge of guilt as I said this, but it entertained Oakley and it was not too far from the truth.

Oakley was quite exuberant that lunchtime. He had, apparently, accomplished a spectacular breakthrough in his study of the insect rectum (to which he had devoted many of his adult years), and was, so he assured me, far ahead of his competitors at Harvard who had developed a multidisciplinary programme of research on the newt bladder. Oakley leaned towards me confidentially. His eyes glistened with excitement.

'I imagine I'm in it,' he hissed.

'In what?'

'The rectum, of course.'

I noticed the Senior Tutor pause in the careful dissection of his crimson-eyed fish and shoot a look in our direction. I had the uneasy feeling that he would make much of that remark in cosy gossip with his cronies. But Oakley was quite oblivious of such things. He went on to explain that his success had resulted from his practice of vividly imagining that he was a water molecule within the locust rectum. I had a fleeting vision of a tiny Oakley, ginger hairs still protruding from his nostrils, floating among moist Gothic columns of living cells seeking the solution to a great mystery concealed among soaring rectal arches. It has an almost Arthurian quality.

Oakley's enthusiasm was singularly depressing, not only because of the subject and method of his studies, but mainly because my own historical research was progressing so slowly. I thought of the untidy manuscript, half buried by unmarked essay papers on my desk. I knew that it was very unlikely that the editor of the *Historical Review* would ever be troubled with a completed version of 'Some Aspects of the Wool Trade in Cricklade, 1536–l546'.

After lunch, I was joined at coffee in the Combination Room by the Senior Tutor. Oakley had left, to rush back to his laboratory to keep an eye on his automatic locust production line. I gathered that if he was not there by two o'clock some unfortunate female insects would be in danger of losing their hindquarters, owing to a mechanical fault which had developed in the apparatus.

The Senior Tutor grumbled about the quality of the candidates for admission to the College and then, as I feared he would, turned the conversation by confessing that he could not help overhearing my talk with Oakley.

'Absolutely fascinating,' he purred, thoughtfully massaging a slightly freckled cheek as he watched me fiddle with one of the College's silver snuff boxes which, for no obvious reason, I had picked up. Playing for time, I grunted, as pleasantly as possible, inexpertly depositing a pile of the pungent brown powder on the back of my hand.

'I didn't quite catch what you said,' he continued. 'Am I to understand that your remarkable interest in natural history is all due to a rather unpleasant old poacher?'

'Yes,' I spluttered in the early stages of asphyxiation.

'Then how did you develop historical interests?'

He knew damned well how I had. It was one of my carefully polished anecdotes. I deployed them quite skilfully when conversation flagged at the High Table.

'Hector . . . my Uncle Hector,' I gasped, still in the grip of the filthy stuff ravaging my nasal passages.

'Ah yes, of course. The distinguished antiquarian from the Wiltshire Downs. I had quite forgotten.'

I resolved to edit my repertoire and, perhaps, cut out some of the stories about my eccentric uncle who had, in truth, lived in a great Tudor house at Ashbourne and, according to my version of events, had laid the foundations of my juvenile interest in history. Pity really, even Molly had laughed at the tales of Uncle Hector. The brassy wife of a visiting American economist had been so enchanted by some of them that she said that I should write a book about it all and suggested that we should both drive down to Ashbourne the next afternoon. However, she mercurially changed her mind at the end of the evening after I had mentioned how much Molly would enjoy the unexpected jaunt. In any case, there would not have been much to see, because the old house had been pulled down – the land that Uncle Hector had called his 'estate' could still, I suppose, be technically described by that term except that it now consisted of several Crescents, Closes and Drives of 1950s bungalows. Looking back, I think that I would quite have enjoyed showing the carefully manicured American blonde my childhood

10

haunts. We could have had tea at the Polly Tea Rooms in Marlborough.

The Senior Tutor left me recovering from his irony and the College snuff to collect his papers for the committee meeting at two o'clock. After he had gone, Chesterton-Hall, a small neat physicist, tried, in his kindly way, to draw me into a conversation he was having with his guest, a large bearded geologist. Chesterton-Hall was speculating whether it would be possible for a helicopter to fly in a very long tube of diameter only slightly larger than that of the rotor blades. I listened with stony incomprehension.

I arrived, late, for the College meeting which was even more dreadful than usual. Two Fellows threatened resignation, as feelings ran high on the vexed question of the continuation of the Research Fellowship in Sanskrit, and another walked out during a protracted argument about the relocation of the undergraduate bicycle sheds.

The supervision with De Freville, at four o'clock, although providing an excuse for escape from the dreadful committee, was the lowest ebb of that grey day. I had carefully prepared my ground and planned to get him to read aloud his essay: 'Effects of the Black Death on Heresy in Late Medieval England'. This strategy had the advantage that it would not only delay the moment when I would be directly exposed to De Freville's supercilious questioning, but would also give me the opportunity to get in a few cutting comments during his exposition. Unfortunately he had not brought his essay with him; he claimed he was now in the process of completely redrafting it to take account of the latest views of Blaylock, very cogently expressed in a recent, important article which De Freville had just come across. He knew very well that, like most other professional historians, I detested

Blaylock and, in any case, would not have seen his latest contribution: I had almost abandoned the regular literature searches of earlier, more enthusiastic days. Furthermore, I was not even sure that there was such an article. I was convinced that De Freville had recently invented a plausible, but non-existent, learned paper to bolster up one of his more baroque arguments. I suspected that De Freville had run into trouble with the topic of the essay and merely chickened out. This suspicion was strengthened when he grumbled that he doubted if there *were* any effects of the Black Death on medieval heresy.

First round to me. I almost relaxed and indulged in a discreet, flirtatious smile at De Freville's fellow supervisee, Sally Emberton, a young lady of large eyes and nice legs, who could still affect my ageing pulse.

Trouble started shortly after I commenced a carefully prepared outline of the essential features of Lollardy. I was still a little rattled by the non-production of De Freville's essay, the reading and criticism of which, I had calculated, would take nearly half an hour. Now I was faced with the alarming prospect of an additional, unguarded period. I felt that I would have welcomed a quiet thirty minutes floating around one of Oakley's rectums searching for some unimportant biological truth. As it was, I sprawled back in a comfortable wing chair in the familiar surrounding of my College room, unaware of the extent of impending disaster. The main thrust of my preamble on Lollardy was the obvious lack of connection between Wycliffe and the humble peasant Lollards. Therein lay my downfall, because it soon became obvious that De Freville had intimate knowledge of an extensive recent literature which showed quite conclusively that run-of-the-mill Lollards were indeed very directly influenced by Wycliffe. For the remainder of the hour,

De Freville pursued me relentlessly, even to the extent of making sarcastic reference to the Black Death and the growth of heresy. I felt like an elderly postmistress being beaten by a sadistic teenage assailant. My humiliation was compounded by Sally's presence, although I seem to remember that, once, she attempted to rally on my behalf, only to be forced to run for cover by De Freville's withering erudition.

At last, one after another, the College clocks clanged out the hour of five o'clock and my torment was over. Before drawing the curtains I looked down at De Freville and Sally hurrying across the wet path which bisected the small brick quad and turned to make myself a cup of instant coffee, in a Worcester cup from the set that Molly had given me years ago when I was first elected to my Fellowship.

I had intended working on the history of the Cricklade wool trade for an hour or so, but failed to raise enough enthusiasm even to remove the unmarked essays. Instead, I poured myself as stiff a whisky as I could from the nearly empty bottle, undid all the misery of tobacco withdrawal, of six weeks earlier, by fishing out a very dry cigar from the box which I had kept on a bookshelf (I suppose for just such an extremity) and sat staring at the gently hissing gas fire, conscious that my toenails needed cutting.

I finally took comfort in another manuscript which I kept safely out of sight in my desk drawer. For nearly a year I had been working on my article: 'The Wading Birds of the Lincolnshire and North Norfolk Marshes'. It was nearly complete and I was already anticipating the pleasure of posting the neatly typed manuscript to the *Lincolnshire Naturalists' Gazette*. I decided to check the entry for *Tringa totanus britannica*. The redshank was my magic bird and I still found myself consoled by the memory of its plaintive call in a wide flat landscape dominated by sea winds and gigantic clouds.

Dinner that night was a solitary meal, for Molly was at her weekly oil painting class. She had left a shepherd's pie, my favourite dish, in the oven: a wifely token of forgiveness for our breakfast row. That, at least, was comforting, as was the familiar flat package, from each end of which protruded the unmistakable type of the weekly newspaper that had chronicled the events of my Wiltshire childhood: marriages and bazaars, my own birth, point-to-point races, my parents' funerals, flower shows, the war, gardening tips and homecomings. Florrie still sent a carefully refolded copy each week, with a declining number of pencilled items for me to read. It was difficult to believe that she was now over seventy: she had come straight from school to my newly married mother to be our timid young housemaid at about the time of the General Strike.

I turned the pages, my mouth full of shepherd's pie, with the usual mixture of nostalgia and boredom. There was so little that meant anything to me now. The fields in which I had roamed (bird's-nesting, exploding empty beer bottles with calcium carbide, finding out what little girls were made of) were now covered with neat streets of suburban houses where cars were washed on Sunday mornings. Even the familiar Wiltshire surnames, Titcombe, Horton, Stratton, seemed to have disappeared. And then, pencilled for my attention, were a few inches of print with a headline that riveted my interest:

ASHBOURNE RELICS PUZZLE EXPERTS

How improbable. After my brush with the Senior Tutor I had almost believed that there had never been such a

14

place. An obscure village quietly snuggling on the edge of chalk downs, overlooking the Vale of the White Horse, sprawling comfortably down from the sound of skylarks into the valley amidst tall trees and scraggy meadows, watercress beds and the calling of moorhens. As I read on, the suppressed memories of half a century before flooded into my mind.

I remembered Uncle Hector in vigorous middle age, tall and erect with a stiff energetic stride and hair that seemed bleached by ancient sunlight. He looked aristocratic and yet invariably dressed like a workman in shabby corduroy trousers, a rough tweed jacket and huge brown boots. His long face, dominated by fierce grey eyes, had an extraordinary, almost frightening intensity.

The hideous De Freville diminished to unimportance as I munched away at Molly's shepherd's pie. The four simple words of that damned newspaper headline had taken me back to a place and time when everything that happened had a heightened significance that nothing since has possessed. For me the 1930s, the years of my childhood, had an intense reality that made all other decades seem flat and grey by comparison, and none flatter than the ten lean years of the tedious carders, combers and staples of sixteenth-century Cricklade. I cursed the tobacco-stained dotard who had led me into that academic *cul-de-sac* in the name of historical respectability. In comparison, even Stanley Baldwin achieved the glamour of a Fred Astaire dancing in bowler hat and white tie through the middle years of that exciting era.

It was as though I had absorbed the spirit of the times with my mother's milk. I could now remember, with astonishing accuracy, fragmentary details from my early childhood, half a century before.

I vividly recalled my first visit to Ashbourne and a dark

wooden door in a high stone wall and the linseed smell of the wood in the summer heat. The door jamb was carved and gouged in a curious repeating pattern. It all came back to me in photographic detail. Above my head was an iron latch, monstrously heavy, which my mother, miraculously, seemed able to move easily with her left hand while I hung grimly to her other one. On the right were double carriage doors, too huge to comprehend.

The carved door opened upon a long straight path of irregular dusty bricks baking in brilliant sunlight and scented air. I could smell the sweetness of drying grass, the perfect, hand-cream smell of roses, the paradoxical freshness of lavender, barely to be recognized as the smell of old ladies and things carefully wrapped in drawers. A straw-hatted, bent old man, his white shirt distorted by a frightening humped back, was swishing away with a large scythe at some stinging nettles. There were bees everywhere dominating the summer hum. Unbelievably, I could see a wooden barn perched on gigantic mushrooms.

We were going to stay with Uncle Hector. I think it was the first time I did so, just before my fifth birthday. I can remember driving out from my home on the outskirts of our town, in the back of a dark blue Austin saloon, bumping along quiet, flinty lanes emblazoned with buttercups and moon daisies, to Ashbourne.

There had been four of us in the car. My father drove, steering carefully along the narrow roads and never driving fast over hump-backed bridges to give a delightful stomach-lifting lurch, which I so enjoyed in my other uncle's car. Grandfather, my mother's father, a gentle twinkling man, bowler-hatted with a white goatee beard, sat next to my father enjoying the passing scene. My mother and I were in the back with our dog, an elderly smooth-coated terrier called Sandy (still smelly from the

16

effects of being cleansed with turpentine, and then soap and water, after I had coloured him green with paint from a conveniently open tin). I was cross and silent. I had been made to wear a cream silk blouse like a lady's, with two mother-of-pearl buttons at each wrist, as well as a pair of hated blue woollen shorts in which I had once wetted myself in public.

My father and grandfather followed behind with our luggage as I trotted, still clutching my mother's hand, along the brick path and turned left to be confronted by another wooden door, this time set in the stone wall of a large, long house which I had not noticed until that moment. This door too was strangely panelled and carved; high up in it was a small square flap which opened to reveal the pale face of a woman. She was wearing rimless spectacles, the first I had ever seen. How was it that the glass did not break?

'Who is it, Bunce?' A man's voice, bossy and rather husky without the familiar and reassuring Wiltshire slurring that my mother called 'common' and which I still find myself striving to suppress.

The flap was abruptly shut, a moment later the heavy door swung open. In the doorway stood the wearer of the rimless glasses, a tall dejected-looking woman, red-nosed and snuffly even in high summer. Behind her, and slightly to her right, stood the owner of the voice and the object of our pilgrimage. I saw him that first time with all the intensity of a small child. Usually, strange adults were grey, anonymous figures, unlit by the fascination evoked by child or dog. Yet this man stood illuminated by my shining interest. I glimpsed a corduroyed leg, fierce grey eyes, a coarse workman's shirt, a bronzed skin marbled with tiny veins around a long, straight nose. He waved to us to enter.

We stepped from the hot garden into a panelled hall which smelled so strongly of apples, wood smoke, cut flowers and old stone that I felt almost tipsy with it. The hall continued as a long shadowy corridor towards the open door of a whitewashed room filled with churns, barrels, sacks, rope and a huge wooden mangle.

Then I can only recall sitting, contentedly swinging my legs, at a green draped table in a pleasant, cream-painted parlour, still bright in late afternoon sunshine. I had been given a glass of cold milk and thin slices of brown bread and butter, liberally spread with honey, which I munched in a happy torpor, gazing at the pink roses which edged the leaded windows.

The memory faded as I finished the shepherd's pie and searched around to find if Molly had left me any pudding. That would be the acid test of reconciliation after our early morning row, for I had a great passion for puddings. There was none. I selected a carton of strawberry yoghurt from the garish row on the second shelf of the refrigerator, pondering on the eroding quality of modern life.

I decided to retire early, not only to extinguish the memory of that unfortunate day, but also to avoid unnecessary confrontation with the evidently only partially reconciled Molly. There was still plenty of time to clear up the kitchen and to smoke another cigar before turning in for the night.

As I inhaled the consoling smoke, I remembered going to bed that first night at Ashbourne House. I was a strange little boy, for I loved going to bed, in an unlighted room, safe and unseen by things outside the window. My bedroom was small, with inadequate, flower-patterned curtains, at the end of a long white corridor. I lay in bed listening to the shrill screams of hawking swifts waiting for the twilight to give way to night.

18

I slept happily in the safety of the protective darkness all alone in the little room at the end of the long empty corridor. However, as I learned much later, things did not go well further down the corridor that night. The fact was that my grandfather, and to a lesser degree my mother (I am still ashamed to say), were rather superstitious. Nothing outlandish, it should be understood, but they showed due caution when faced with new moons, black cats, lilac in the house, broken mirrors and nocturnal bumpings. Now, as I was also later to learn, my Uncle Hector's house was old, very old – Tudor in fact. What is more, there were plenty of stories in the village about it being haunted. My uncle's hump-backed gardener (who was terrifying enough for me even in broad daylight) had evidently also regaled my grandfather with a lurid account of a ghost and, particularly, of the involvement of a skeleton which, he said, lay in the room with three steps, at the top of the narrow staircase leading from the hall.

While I was sleeping so soundly in the little whitewashed room at the end of the corridor, my grandfather was having a series of appalling experiences in the next room but one to mine. These commenced, at the customary midnight hour, with sliding noises in the darkness. Then the counterpane moved, apparently of its own volition. Finally, my poor grandfather's fear was compounded by the strange behaviour of our dog, Sandy, who had been assigned to him for protection, but in fact initiated the most terrifying part of the whole proceedings. As I later learned (for it became part of family history), Sandy had woken suddenly 'with every hair on his body standing straight up' (probably because my grandfather lit a candle) and backed away, staring fixedly at the seemingly empty space near the end of Grandfather's bed. After this the dog was reputed to have kept an invisible spot accurately in focus as he walked, growling or whining (I can't remember which), to the locked bedroom door. Whatever 'it' was supposedly proceeded back to the skeleton's room.

I was unaware of the contents of that room, or of my grandfather's nocturnal adventures, and awoke to the sound of bird song and early morning sunshine. I peered out of the little window to see, at the side of the house, the wooden barn with it supporting mushrooms. To my delight my grandfather, whom I dearly loved, and who normally rose late, came to my room with Sandy, and the three of us crept out into the morning dew before anyone else stirred in the great silent house.

This was my first exploration of Uncle Hector's estate. We found at the back of the house an untidy, cobbled courtyard leading to glorious pyramids of colour: two square flower beds, in the old country style, edged with London Pride and marigolds, and within them dahlias with gigantic sunflowers rearing up at the centre. We walked along a grassy path between the towering fragrant colours which were already alive with bees. Then we found ourselves amidst tall straight rows of scarlet runners, bulging marrows and blackcurrant bushes, all edged with dew. We pushed open a rickety slatted gate into an alarmingly steep field of buttercups and great scraggy clumps of nettles, made secret by a huge surrounding hedge, tall trees and the absent-minded calling of wood pigeons. From here we turned left into a long, grassy paddock, occupied by two very dangerous-looking goats. Through yet another gate we came to the untidy expanse of grass at the front of the house, from where I could see fresh wonders, which I had not noticed on arrival – a large orchard, partly hidden by a rampant elder hedge, and a circular pond which I would have to explore for frogs. I cannot recall what happened next, but I suppose I must have been washed and given my breakfast. However, I distinctly remember the relief of being ignored as the grown-ups talked in that queer, affected way which, in other adults, my mother called 'putting it on'. Even my Uncle Hector was taking part, announcing something incomprehensible in a loud authoritative voice. To me, now able to observe in safety for the first time, he looked very fierce. It would certainly not take much to make him cross. His hair was much longer than that of either my father or my grandfather, who shared a fanatical preference for short back and sides (a fate from which I knew my mother was still trying to protect my childish locks).

I also watched Miss Bunce, who, strangely, and unlike *our* maid Florrie, seemed actually to live in the house. She was overawed by Uncle Hector – you could see that. She seemed mostly to lurk in the scullery, with the gigantic mangle, and only emerged to hover discreetly in the background. Her hands were rough ('spreethed', according to Wiltshire patois). I could see that she was a droopy long-suffering kind of woman.

While the grown-ups were 'putting it on' I slipped out to explore – this time inside the house. From the parlour, I crossed the dark panelled hall into another gloomy corridor to find a room filled with enormous chairs and dominated by an open fireplace, nearly as high as the ceiling, still piled with ashes and a half burned log. Beyond was yet another door, conveniently half open. I peered in to discover the largest room I had ever seen. It too was panelled and smelt of stale wood smoke. On three sides were leaded windows, through which I could glimpse the brilliant summer roses, isolated from the silent, dusty scene. In the middle a long table was loaded with piles of books, heaps of papers and several blue-and-white pots. This was too much to comprehend. As I retreated I noticed *another* staircase, I supposed where Uncle Hector and Miss Bunce slept, but I certainly wasn't going to risk going up there.

And then boredom and loneliness descended together. I decided to find my way to my bedroom, there to have a quiet sniff at the fine hairs on the back of my arm (a very comforting activity, which, unaccountably, infuriated my father). When I reached the top of the staircase from the hall I stopped at the three steps leading to a white door, the only painted one in the house, with a polished brass handle and a large keyhole. The door was locked. When I peeped through the keyhole I could only see the side of a table and, on top, a long glass case, but I could not make out what was in it.

I recalled all this with perfect clarity; forgotten things revived by Florrie's pencilled marks in the carefully folded copy of the *North Wilts Herald and Advertiser*. I knew only too well those relics which puzzled the experts at Ashbourne and which were now, no doubt, already numbered and catalogued before being locked away on dusty shelves. The memory of them, so recently dug from the chalky soil, had haunted my childhood days and now brought vivid fresh recollection. I turned off my bedside light at the sound of Molly's car turning into the drive and once again sought refuge in protective darkness.

2

Looking back, I think that I must have been a very nice little boy. Life had not been soured by disappointment, although difficult times lay ahead and would be made more so by my strange uncle.

Not long after our visit to Uncle Hector's, my grandfather died. Not that my mother ever used that word: Grandpa had 'passed away'. How this happened I never knew and was so upset afterwards that I never wanted to know. All I remember is being removed from my bed, hastily washed and taken out for the day by our neighbour and her husband. This I didn't like at all because, although they were kind to me, we had to spend most of the day on a quite inexplicable 'drive round' (as such local car journeys were termed). I was also worried at their practice of tearing the *North Wilts Herald and Advertiser* down the middle so that each could read a page simultaneously. The *Advertiser* was a sacred journal in my home, to be read very carefully, first by Grandfather then by Father and lastly by my mother, and certainly not to be torn in half under any circumstances whatever.

It was when I returned that I was told that my grandfather had passed away. It took me some time to realize that this meant dead. I could not comprehend the loss but tried to comfort myself with the thought that Grandfather would certainly by now be in heaven, wearing his bowler hat, probably reading an intact edition of the *North Wilts Herald and Advertiser*.

Shortly after the loss of Grandfather, my friendship blossomed with Tessy, a little girl who lived on the other side of the brick wall at the end of our garden. Unfortunately it was so high that we were forced to balance, to our great peril, on our own sides to communicate directly. Tessy, somewhat older than me, hit on the stratagem of loosening one of the bricks in the wall so as eventually to extract it and thus provide a sort of oblong port-hole to facilitate our developing social life. After much effort we gained our objective. However, soon after the achievement, which left us both covered in brick dust, I witnessed a totally unexpected and disturbing phenomenon on the other side of the wall. One day, shortly after she had withdrawn the loose brick, and I had applied my eye to the aperture, Tessy provided a spontaneous and very explicit display which left no doubt that little girls were very different indeed from little boys. Furthermore, it was borne on me what girls, and even more embarrassing, *ladies*, did when they went to the lavatory. I had not even considered the possibility before and still found it difficult to imagine those beautiful, scented beings doing such a thing. As for respectable old ladies, it didn't bear thinking about.

To make matters very much worse, my mother chose this time to shift me from the tiny bedroom which I had occupied since I was a baby into the much larger one previously used by my grandfather. I was to sleep in his bed. Even protective darkness was of little help to a small worried boy, trying not to think of what had happened in that very bed only a few weeks before. It was, therefore, with some relief that I learned that we were, again, to stay with my Uncle Hector. He was very kind to us on that visit. He seemed different. For one thing, he spoke to me quite often. Once he ruffled my hair and said that I was a good chap. However, he could still look very fierce and on at least one occasion became very cross indeed.

The matter concerned the dogs that he had recently acquired – to give warning, I gathered, against intruders. There were two dogs. One was black and what Uncle Hector called a lurcher; the other was small, white and very hairy, possibly a variety of Sealyham. The dogs were tied up. The trouble was that they would keep escaping. When Uncle Hector walked round to where they were kept, there would be a length of chewed-off rope or a slipped collar still attached to a chain. And then there would be much shouting by my uncle, and the dog or dogs, would be sought. We were all mobilized for the search. Even Miss Bunce was summoned from the scullery and the hunchback forced to abandon his perpetual scything. When an escapee was caught, the ritual was always the same, and; to me, quite awful. The poor dog was tied up on a very short chain and just whacked and whacked by my uncle with a thick cudgel. I am sure that the chastisement was heard for miles. It was not just the roaring of my uncle and the great whacking noise but, most of all, the yelping of the dogs ('chi-iking' we used to call it). Then I used to run away in floods of tears to my mother begging her to stop Uncle Hector from doing such a terrible thing. But she never would and made some excuse even though I was sure she knew it was wrong. If I had been bigger I would have killed him.

After all the pandemonium was over, I would creep round behind the hedge where the dogs were tethered for their beatings, having first made sure that there was no sign of Uncle Hector. It was worse when the little white dog was beaten. He used to whimper for hours and would cry out even when I touched him gently. I used to take them water and pieces of stolen meat and worried about

25

them most of the time – as if I didn't really have enough on my mind, what with Tessy's revelations and my grandfather's bed and wondering what they had done with his body.

I could tell that my father didn't like the dog beatings either, but he never said anything to Uncle Hector and certainly did not fight him as I would have liked to have done. I was very glad we had not brought Sandy with us.

After the beatings everyone seemed quiet and deflated. Miss Bunce crept around in an even more subdued manner than usual and seemed to become more friendly with my mother. My father went fishing and Uncle Hector lurked in the long dusty room with the books, which, I learned, was called the library (I found this very difficult to connect with the place of the same name in our town where my mother went to change her Netta Muskett books on Friday evenings).

By this time I was becoming quite familiar with Uncle's estate and I ventured to the furthermost limits without undue anxiety, except, of course, for the goats. Fierce and unpredictable, they seemed all too appropriate for my uncle. The main trouble was that they got moved around and occasionally I would blunder upon them. Then it was usually a question of hanging on to the horns of whichever one was first encountered while I bellowed for adult assistance. Once when I was in this terrifying predicament, I caught a glimpse of my uncle looking out of his library window and I am sure that he was laughing. He certainly did not come to release me on that occasion.

I began to explore the house, even timidly penetrating into the dusty sunlight of the library when no one was about. The only room I had not seen was the one behind the locked white door at the top of the staircase.

My uncle soon abandoned his library studies and, to

my surprise, was positively benign. He even made me an accomplice in a project that he had been contemplating for some time and which I subsequently incorporated into my repertoire of 'Uncle Hector stories'. This, like so many others, had arisen from one of his ungovernable rages. I had not noticed, until he pointed it out to me, that a small brick bungalow had been built exactly opposite the entrance in the front wall. I thought that it looked quite pretty. My uncle did not and was particularly incensed when the owners had the temerity to appear in their garden, where they could be clearly seen from the opened wall door. He had, therefore, invented a device which would prevent the interlopers from seeing his roof and chimney pots, should they chance to look up in that direction. The device consisted of a series of vertical wooden poles which were erected with great difficulty (by a very tall workman in brown overalls and a large cap), on top of my uncle's already very high wall. The poles were topped with a long, flat piece of wood to which were attached some pulleys and a rope. A number of sheep hurdles were then suspended from the rope and could be moved back and forth by operating the pulleys. In this way Uncle Hector could obscure such glimpses of his property as his neighbours might, with considerable difficulty, snatch above the wall. The scheme initially gave uncle the tremendous pleasure of opening the wall door, glaring across at the bungalow and then adjusting the positions of the hanging sheep hurdles according to the exact position of his unwelcome neighbours at any particular time. But he soon got bored with the operation and this is where I came in. It was my job to be what Uncle called his 'scout' (no doubt chosen to recall military operations in the Boer War). This involved me in regularly reporting to Uncle Hector the disposition of his adversaries. He would then come with me and fiddle with the pulleys until the hurdles were deployed to maximum effect. The only trouble was that I was unable to operate the latch in the wall door. It was too heavy and too high for me. However, I did not wish to reveal my inadequacies more than was necessary and so would crawl through a very thick hedge further up the road, nip down to carry out my observations and then return by the same route.

I was so grateful to Uncle Hector for involving me in what I considered to be a very noble scheme, that I was almost prepared to try to forget the dog beatings. He was also, as I could now see, rather handsome in an elderly sort of way. My reservations about him were further eroded when he gave me a conducted tour of the estate. Father had left (he had to go back to work) so I was grateful for my uncle's attentions, although still feeling distinctly vulnerable. I desperately wanted him to like me for, despite his strange behaviour towards his dogs, he seemed simultaneously god-like and very manly, as I imagined a soldier would be.

I was shown so many things that my mind reeled. In some long, flint-walled buildings there were several church pulpits. He let me climb up one of them and I stood inside overwhelmed by the smell of old wood. Behind two wide doors was a most impressive motor car, grey, with much brass work – identified, intriguingly, as a 'bull-nose'. In odd corners were piles of pikes and old swords. Uncle Hector picked up a small, rusty one with a solid brass handle and handed it to me. It took me some moments to realize that it was a gift and that I was now the owner of such a totally delightful object. It was while standing with the sword in my hand, wondering what my mother would have to say about it, that I noticed a pair of jagged steel jaws hanging on the whitewashed wall by a length of black chain.

'Man-trap', my uncle replied to my unspoken question. And that was that.

3

I must admit that I was badly rattled by the arrival of Florrie's pencilled copy of the *North Wilts Herald and Advertiser*; so much so, that on the following morning I decided to take the day off. This was not difficult, for I had intended going to London, to work in the Public Record Office and, later, to attend a lecture (rather from duty than interest) on Tudor agriculture by George Anstey, at University College. I had rearranged my teaching, so it would be easy for me to bolt up to the Norfolk coast.

I felt that a few hours on those lonely salt marshes might calm me. It would certainly give me the chance to think things out and would provide an opportunity for reconciliation with Molly, who, I knew, wanted t make some sketches for a large marine landscape that she had in mind.

Molly fell in with my plan with surprise, and some gratitude, at my unexpected thoughtfulness.

We had a pub lunch. Afterwards, I left Molly perched on a sea wall happily filling the pages of her pad with sketches of sea holly, muddy creeks and towering clouds. It was low tide when I started out. There was plenty to see: several flocks of bar-tailed godwits, two hen-harriers and a short-eared owl hunting low over the marshes.

The tide started running back at about four o'clock. As I turned along the edge of a filling creek I realized the strangeness of my situation – driven to that lonely place by events of nearly fifty years before. I kicked over a bundle of white bones and tattered sandy feathers that had once been the corpse of an oiled razorbill. As a child I had been obsessed with animal skeletons.

I can't remember when I started to keep an animal ossuary. I was fascinatated by the white perfection of the tiny bones and enjoyed the jackdaw pleasure of possessing them and the challenge of trying to piece them together. I was helped by my only real grown-up friend, Darkie Hurrell. It was he who had contributed such rarities as the stoat and badger skulls. I suppose that Darkie was a strange friend for a little boy, but he was a central figure in my early life, which I now realize was a lonely one. He lived a couple of miles from my home in a small brick cottage, with a grey slate roof and black tarred walls, beside a deep wood that was soon to be obliterated by the advancing line of smart villas which continually threatened the dusty rural edges of the town.

Darkie Hurrell was a regular visitor to our house. He never knocked or called out, but would just appear silently, in kitchen or garden, to await a greeting. He was tall, with dark skin, black hair flecked with white and a full walrus moustache. He had large, brown eyes with which I believed that he could see in the darkest places. His clothes were, to my eyes, unusual and old fashioned: the jacket was long with buttons all the way down the front and vast pockets with buttoned flaps. He always wore a large cap, made of a grey material with a herring-bone pattern, invariably adorned with a rabbit's foot, which he said was his badge of office.

My father loved to 'yarn' with Darkie Hurrell in the kitchen where they would sit smoking and drinking beer from two enormous brown mugs. Their talk was of animals, country characters and the seasons. Rarely did they speak of the present. Usually their gossip was of times long ago, clearly remembered and carefully recounted.

Darkie never set foot further into the house than the scullery or kitchen. He greeted my mother, when she appeared, with elaborate courtesy and would often produce a ragged bunch of flowers for her: cowslips, bluebells, primroses, dog roses, depending on the season. Darkie was unmarried and lived in what must have been some discomfort on his smallholding. He always seemed hungry and would demolish cold puddings, lumps of cake, pies, bread and cheese – anything that was going.

My mother pretended to disapprove of Darkie Hurrell, but I think that she was flattered by his compliments and happy that he should amuse her husband and her only son. However, one Christmas morning she was very cross indeed when Darkie appeared, the worse for drink, carefully shaved and with his hair greased down, wearing a woman's necklace. I was fascinated by his jewellery. It consisted of a fine golden chain and numerous blue – I suppose glass – jewels. It really looked very pretty. But his appearance angered my mother who was busy with the Christmas dinner at the time. Her anger increased still further when it was discovered, after Darkie's departure, that *every one* of our pile of mince pies had disappeared.

Despite his depredations, Darkie made significant and regular contributions to our household economy. These we would awake to find tied to the handle of our back door: rabbits, or a hare, or a brace of pheasants or, occasionally, a pike or some trout.

Darkie was good at hanging things on door knobs. My father was very amused by the story, which he told repeatedly, of how Darkie Hurrell had once confounded the nature correspondent of the *North Wilts Herald and*

Advertiser. As I recall the affair, the newspaper had published an article stating 'on the highest authority' that some particularly rare bird of prey was now extinct in North Wiltshire. Darkie's reply was decisive: he shot a specimen of the extinct creature and hung it on the front door knob of the newspaper office.

Darkie Hurrell was a marvellous antidote to the worries that beset me at that time: my grandfather's corpse, the disturbing glimpses of Tessy, Uncle Hector's terrible dog beatings and the bodily functions of ladies. He would talk about animals and how to catch them. A particular treat was to be allowed to look at, and handle, his double-barrelled shotgun. This he carried in two parts in his jacket: the stock in one capacious inside pocket and the barrel in the other. The stock was dark, lovingly polished and shod with brass. The trigger and guard were kept bright with oil. The barrels were also carefully oiled and could easily be clicked into the stock to form a beautiful and deadly weapon.

A much less welcome treat was to be handed one of the ferrets that Darkie would sometimes extract from the right-hand pocket of his jacket. Both Sandy and I regarded these lithe little animals with considerable trepidation. The thought of their small sharp teeth sinking into the quivering neck of a frightened rabbit became another of my obsessional worries.

Perhaps the strangest of Darkie's personal possessions was the bronze bracelet that he wore on his left wrist. It was shaped like a flattened horseshoe with small knobs at each end. Darkie said that he found the bracelet sticking from the chalky earth of a ploughed field and that it was Roman. It not only brought him luck, but kept him free from rheumatism.

Later Darkie found another ancient ornament in

33

another corner of the same field. It too was bronze, about three inches long, T-shaped and reeded with a scroll top. Darkie cleaned the brooch and polished it so that the decorations could be seen. Then he carefully wrapped it in a clean white handkerchief and put it in his left-hand pocket, walked the two miles to our home and there shyly took it out and put it into my Mother's hand. My mother was mystified by the gift, it was so old and strange, but she was grateful and forgave Darkie his sins with the mince pies. However, she rarely wore the brooch. The only times I can remember her doing so were when we visited Uncle Hector. I suspect she wore it on purpose to intrigue him, for she would never tell how she got it. But he knew that it was Roman and said that my mother should have given it to a museum. Mother eventually lost the brooch and now I can hardly remember its design.

Darkie Hurrell had a wonderful store of country skills. He could catch trout in a nearby lake by dropping grasshoppers on the surface and shooting the fish between the eyes with a 0.22 rifle as they rose to investigate the struggling insects. Pheasants he caught with rat traps, baited with peas; or else he waited for them with his shotgun, concealed at one end of his long row of neglected runner beans. He knew how to set a snare to catch a rabbit with absolute certainty and how to knock over a hare on misty autumn nights.

The most wonderful thing that Darkie Hurrell did for me happened early one summer morning. I was still in bed and my mother called me down. Hurrell had something for me. And there in his great hand was a tiny squeaking scrap of fluffy feathers dominated by a gaping yellow beak.

34

'It's for you, Master James,' Darkie laughed, 'a jack-daw chick.'

This ball of feathers turned out to be a great responsibility. I was kept constantly busy poking food into its gaping beaky void, but it grew and grew and soon I had the best pet anyone could have wished for – a pet that followed me everywhere and left a trail of havoc that I found most satisfying.

My uncle Hector inspected my new pet on one of his occasional calls to our home. He was not particularly impressed, largely, I recall, because he had been lashing himself into one of his periodic furies. This time he was incensed by the activities of a small bespectacled Indian, dressed in a white sheet, who had visited the local railway workshop and who, if not dealt with, would bring down the British Empire. My uncle wanted only one thing: 'Five minutes with a horse whip in a loose box with the little swine.' (I later learned that this was his standard fantasy about any public figure who incurred his wrath, notably the Communist MP, Willie Gallacher, and Hewlett Johnson, the 'Red Dean'.)

Despite many obvious differences, Uncle Hector and Darkie Hurrell had certain traits in commmon. They both dressed in the same way, in multi-buttoned and many pocketed tweed jackets. They both just appeared in our house, without knocking or calling out: Uncle Hector in the front parlour, and nowhere else, and Darkie Hurrell in the scullery and kitchen, and no further. They were both bringers of gifts from the countryside; Uncle Hector's were, however, decidedly the more stingy and, oddly enough, that is how he wanted it to appear. He would fish about in a pocket and pull out a handful of maggoty, wrinkled apples, gruffly announcing: 'Brought some windfallers.'

It was usually I who would discover Uncle Hector pacing about our front parlour. He seemed to fill the room with his presence and was always engaged in the minute examination of our Staffordshire figures or our George Morland prints or my aunt Flossie's oil paintings. Then he would thrust a crumpled paper bag at me – 'Brought a few pullet's eggs.'

Odd that I should have remembered that after all those years. I am something of a standing joke in the College for my forgetful habits. Oakley maintains that it is part of my pose as the absent-minded don. Molly knew better. I found a bad-tempered and very cold wife awaiting me in gathering dusk on the sea wall. I could tell from two hundred yards, and in failing light, that she was cross with me, just as I could with my mother as a small boy.

I drove back in chilly silence, conscious that I had still not marked those damned essays.

4

The trip to the Norfolk coast was not a success. Yet I had been thrilled to see the hunting short-eared owl and Molly became more affable after supper, which I cooked – another attempt at reconciliation. I wrote up my field notes, chatted with Molly about her next painting and then slipped off to bed. I was feeling tired after all that squelching, in heavy wading boots, across so many miles of muddy creeks, saltings and drains. But sleep would not come and I kept thinking of Uncle Hector as he was when I was nearly six years old. It was astonishingly clear to me.

I remembered how I wondered about what he actually did. After all, most other adults seemed to have clearly-defined jobs which housed, clothed and sustained them and their families. Uncle Hector, on the other hand, lived in what we thought was considerable splendour and seemed to follow no recognizable trade or profession.

It took some years for my childish mind to piece together the things I heard. First I discovered that Uncle Hector was not an uncle at all; he was in fact my mother's cousin. I also learned that, although he was 'better off' than we were, things had not always been that way. In fact, his side of the family had evidently been a notch or two below ours. They had been 'in' second-hand furniture, definitely not of the status of *our* business, a proper furniture firm with several staff, workshops and *two* vans, which had been founded by my great-grandfather in 1840.

Uncle Hector had evidently been quite a lad in his

young days. He had left for the Boer War (in the Imperial Yeomanry) with thirty pounds in his pocket and had returned a wealthy man, at least by our modest standards, able to buy himself the Tudor house on the edge of the Downs and to do not a stroke of useful work from that day forward. My mother had no idea how Uncle Hector had acquired his wealth. Father used to mutter something about 'i.d.b.', but Mother would always hush him and tell him not to say such silly things. It was not until many years later that I realized that my father meant Illegal Diamond Buying. Uncle Hector had not been commissioned during the Boer War. This surprised me, because he looked to me to be very aristocratic and I could not imagine him as an ordinary trooper. Evidently something very dramatic and unusual had happened to Uncle Hector in that distant war. This made him a still more mysterious, even dangerous, figure, very different from the familiar business associates of my father and certainly from the few poverty-stricken farmers who were our immediate social circle.

Uncle Hector had had a younger brother, Hert, a happy-go-lucky young man, much liked by my mother, who had been killed on the Somme in 1916. His mother and father had also died, so that Uncle Hector was left on his own with my mother and her brother, my most favourite uncle, David, as his only kin. Uncle Hector had quarrelled with Uncle David, and so we were the only family that he had. Miss Bunce, my mother very carefully emphasized, was not 'family', she was only my uncle's housekeeper. Neither were the two rather pretty, fair-haired ladies who occasionally spent some time at Uncle Hector's house. They were secretaries who came to help from time to time. My mother grew quite cross when I said that I had never seen them doing any typing for

Uncle Hector. In fact, I hadn't even seen a typewriter. Anyway it didn't matter, my mother said, because they would not be helping him again.

The most fascinating thing about Uncle Hector was what my mother called his 'hobby'. It was glorified with a totally unpronounceable name which I only mastered some years later: archaeology. This was the reason for the curious collections of objects in the flint-walled out-buildings, the piles of books in the library and the locked white door at the top of the stairs. My mother certainly did not regard Uncle Hector's archaeological activities with undue respect. To her they were just another mascu-line eccentricity, like my father's fishing, or philately, or even my own bone-collecting. In a curious way Uncle Hector's scholarship irritated her, particularly when he spoke of his visits to a wealthy landowner who lived in a very grand manor across the Downs and who shared uncle's antiquarian interests. To her, this was just 'swank-ing'. I think that Mother could not believe that anyone from our family could be friendly with such grand people or could be anything but an amateur. Reality consisted of the furniture business, farming and other kindred, practi-cal trades. Real scholars were remote figures working at places like Oxford University which my mother had glimpsed during very occasional shopping trips; she had not the remotest idea of what went on there. I understood and accepted her attitude. After all, I knew only too well that my own humble bone collection was a childish thing and that one day I would be faced with the daunting prospect of earning my own living.

Nevertheless, I was excited when I realized that my uncle knew about things that happened in the remote past, of the Romans and, in particular, of the people who had lived up on the Downs in the ancient grassy fortresses

39

which my father used to tell me about when we went for Sunday afternoon drives. It began to dawn on me that it would be fun to dig and poke about in the chalky soil and discover exciting things of the sort Darkie Hurrell found. There might even be swords and golden crowns.

My next visit to Uncle Hector's was therefore made with a pleasant sense of expectation, despite the sadness of leaving my jackdaw and Sandy to the care of my father, who did not stay with us on that visit. I was also looking forward to the prospect of sailing my clockwork ocean liner, an unexpected present from my father. It had a real propeller, an adjustable rudder and a key that could be pushed down the middle of the three funnels and twisted to produce a very satisfying clicking sound as the spring tightened within the little tin-plate ship.

At first things went very well. My new-found curiosity and enthusiasm for the antique were rewarded by my uncle who told me interesting stories and even took me into the long, dusty library. It was on that occasion that he gave me a battered leather book, with one cover torn right off. I still have it: *Stories of Robin Hood and His Merry Outlaws, retold from the old ballads* by J. Walker McSpadden, published in 1909 by George G. Harrap and Company. I could not read it at the time, but I gazed at the pictures and got my mother to read the legends: how Robin Hood was buried 'near to the fair Kirkleys', of 'Nottingham in the days of Robin Hood' and of Robin himself as 'he drew the bow back to his ear'.

Later, I was told, I would be taken to see Uncle's museum, although my mother looked distinctly anxious at this suggestion. Late in the afternoon I was taken up the staircase and watched as the white door was unlocked by my uncle who seemed to relish the prospect of taking me into the forbidden territory. Actually, it was very disappointing. The walls were lined with pots and bits of broken pottery, all in glass cases. The only interesting thing was the skeleton in a glass case in the middle of the room. I would have liked it for my collection.

After this high point, the visit deteriorated badly. First, one of Uncle Hector's dogs, the small white one, slipped his collar and escaped. Miss Bunce brought the dreadful news, which roused my uncle to instant fury. We were all dispatched to different points of my uncle's little kingdom to search for the fugitive. Miraculously, as it seemed, *I* found the dog, or rather he found me – in the far corner of the orchard. I spoke to the quivering creature, petted him and then had the bright idea of taking him back to the chain and putting on his collar. I would not say anything, so that when Uncle Hector noticed the dog back in its proper place he might think that Bunce had been mistaken and would not beat the wretched animal. But he did and, as usual, I was devastated by the yelping and the thudding of the great stick.

Things went a little better the next day, Whit Monday, 1934 (I know the date because, on the day before, my uncle wrote in the Robin Hood book in his neat hand: 'To James Yeo, Whit Sunday 1934'). The trouble happened at what I had hoped would be a glorious moment: the launching of my clockwork liner. The ship had just completed its maiden voyage across my uncle's circular pond and I was happily winding it up for the second trip when a shadow passed across me as I knelt at the water's edge. It was Uncle Hector.

'What have you got there, boy?'

I handed him my precious possession, still worried, confused and unsure of my attitude to him after the recent dog-beating episode. He took it and turned it round, examining it minutely, first looking at the bows

41

and then at the white, tinny superstructure and funnels. Finally, his eyes reached the stern and spied the words 'Foreign Made'. With a single roar he flung my lovely liner as far as he could into a vast bed of stinging nettles, which had escaped the labours of the hunchback. 'Foreign rubbish,' he bawled and then turned on his heels, leaving me weeping at the side of the pool.

I went into the orchard and hid in the hollow hedge at the far end. I felt like the little whipped dog and wanted to be alone with my humiliation. After a time I suppressed my grief sufficiently to search for the little tin liner. It was nearly dusk when I found it. I was by then horribly stung and could not find any dock leaves to soothe the pain.

And still my sufferings were not over, for we had a cooked supper that evening. I watched with horror as my uncle piled my plate with slices of fatty meat and cabbage. I could not eat fat or cabbage, they just would not go down to back of my throat. I tried and failed. Soon everyone else had clean plates. Then my tormentor decreed that I should not leave the table until I had cleared my plate. So I sat for what seemed like ages gazing at congealing fat and cold cabbage through tear-filled eyes. I was eventually released by Bunce and my mother who whisked me from the table and up to my bedroom. Shortly after, I could hear my uncle shouting at poor Bunce for her unexpected act of defiance.

Mother and I left next morning, when my father came to collect us. I was never so pleased to see Sandy and Jack and to be away from that terrible place which had once seemed so infinitely desirable.

5

Perhaps because of the appalling Whitsuntide of 1934, I was not taken to my uncle's house for the remainder of the summer. When he called at our home, I made myself scarce. However, I learned that things were afoot between Uncle Hector and my father. It appeared that Uncle Hector intended to drive to a place called St Albans, a very long way from Wiltshire, there, in my mother's words, 'to dig up Roman remains'. It was proposed that Father should accompany Uncle Hector to help with the digging. They were to go in my uncle's 'bull-nose' and were to camp at this place.

Father seemed to be quite excited by the prospect of an unexpected archaeological jaunt. Despite my recent painful encounters with Uncle Hector I too was pleased that my father was going on something which sounded so important. I was, in fact, very proud of my father, despite some reservations largely connected with an uncomfortably abrasive chin and pungent tobacco smells. I was particularly impressed that he had been an officer in the Great War, and often used to play surreptitiously with a wicked-looking French bayonet, a Very Light pistol, a bugle and a steel helmet which had been carefully hidden beneath some blankets, in the bottom drawer of a chest, to escape my attentions. His three medals, which he called 'Pip, Squeak and Wilfred' and kept in his tie drawer, were also cherished objects that I regularly fished out to admire when the coast was clear.

The preparations for the St Albans expedition were

43

fascinating. My father's army camp-bed was taken out from under the stairs and added to a growing accumulation of objects including a camping kettle, primus stove, our frying pan, ground sheet, Wellington boots, a large box camera and tins of bully beef. Uncle Hector was to provide an old army tent in which they would both sleep.

I kept out of the way when Uncle Hector's large grey car drove up to be loaded and managed to take a shy farewell of my father behind the grandfather clock (so as not to be seen in an obvious demonstration of affection).

The house seemed empty without my father and I was therefore pleased when Darkie Hurrell paid one of his regular visits. I was cast down again, however, when he told me that things were hard with him. It was some time since he had 'had a good bag'.

I spent much of the time training and playing with my jackdaw. Each morning he would fly up to my window and tap on the glass with his beautiful black beak. I would let him in and he would come to the bathroom with me, before being routinely expelled by my mother. He could do fabulous things such as calling the dog (who was usually fooled), taking the pegs out of my mother's washing and pecking Florrie's toes.

I had been playing with Jack when I came into the house to hear, to my intense surprise, Father talking to my mother in the parlour. He sounded angry and I, as was my custom, listened outside the door. I quickly learned that it had rained very heavily at St Albans, especially on the previous night, and that my uncle had taken along a barrel of beer. And then my blood froze when I heard my father exclaim: 'Then he *peed* in my Wellington boot and, what is more, laughed when I shouted at him.' Now the word that my father had used was a very rude one, at least to small boys of sheltered

44

upbringing in North Wiltshire in late 1934. I sometimes still blushed at the memory of the nurse, in the hospital where I had my tonsils out, who had asked whether I wanted to have a 'pee'. And that is what Uncle Hector had done in my father's Wellington boot. It was absolutely awful. I was not surprised to hear Father say that he had walked out there and then and found his own way back, by train, from St Albans and, what is more, had finished with my mother's precious cousin.

I was full of indignation at this latest outrage. Dog beating, toy liner throwing and now *this*. It was too much.

I was later given a bowdlerized version of the St Albans affair and told how my father had had a disagreement with Uncle Hector. Relations were now to be totally severed.

Yet we still managed to hear news of his doings. A few weeks after the St Albans outrage we received a call from Sid Thorpe. Sid was an upright man of military bearing. He invariably wore a flat, ginger tweed cap, had gold-rimmed spectacles and carried a silver-topped walking stick. Brisk was the word for Sid Thorpe. He had long been a close friend of Uncle Hector and regularly walked the eight miles out to the village for a gossip and a drink. Yet on his last call he had been accused of some unspecified treachery and had been shown off the premises.

The next news came from an unexpected visit by Miss Bunce who had caught the bus into town to do some shopping and called in for a chat with my mother. She looked tired, had her usual cold and was loaded with a heavy shopping basket. My mother, who was not normally 'keen' on Miss Bunce, seemed quite pleased to see Uncle Hector's long-suffering housekeeper. As far as I could make out (for I still found most adult conversation singularly dull and difficult to follow) Uncle Hector was in excellent fettle and was, in fact, at that very moment, busily engaged on a project to dig out some carved Roman stones that he had found near Cricklade and planned to reassemble on his own land. It sounded so interesting that I felt acute pangs of regret that direct communications had been severed with Uncle Hector. However, the violation of my father's Wellington boot was clearly an insuperable obstacle, quite apart from the act of imperial piracy on my toy liner and the outrageous attempt to force fat and cabbage on me. It was all very difficult and I still could not understand why the most interesting grown-up whom I had ever met (and that included Darkie Hurrell) should behave in such a peculiar way. Beneath all my confusion and bruised loyalties. I suppose that I still longed to be accepted by him and to take part in some glorious feats of archaeological dis- covery, preferably coupled with some suitably safe acts of juvenile heroism that would re-establish me in my uncle's affections as a jolly good chap and a credit to the British Empire.

However, my heroism was soon to be taxed in another direction, for arrangements had been made for the first formal stages of my education. With great apprehension, I learned that I was shortly to be sent to Selhurst House School for Girls and Boys. I remember, vividly, the mental picture that the first mention of this educational establishment conjured up in my mind. I saw a vast room, full of lines of desks policed by sinister figures dressed in black gowns and mortar boards – a scene compounded from God knows what juvenile picture books. In reality, Selhurst House School for Girls and Boys turned out to be a large suburban house in a leafy avenue not far from my own home. The staff consisted of the proprietors,

Miss Dora and Miss Daisy, and a downtrodden young lady whom I like instantly. I did not like Miss Dora, who I soon discovered was permanently armed with a very painful weapon in the shape of an ancient ebony ruler; I was reserving my judgment about Miss Daisy who, although severe-looking, did produce, in the middle of the morning, some delicious bars of homemade coconut ice and glasses of hot milk – at a halfpenny a piece. I definitely did *not* like the female Mafia, consisting of some older girls (notably Patsy Bailey and Barbara Thorne) who roughed me up behind a large laurel bush at the end of the garden which served as our playground. However, I was comforted by some much needed succour, in the form of a sticky boiled sweet, produced (from a secret pocket in a pair of grubby blue knickers) by Diana Huck.

Going to school was a distressing enough experience; worse was to come. One autumnal Sunday afternoon I received another severe setback when my father and I walked across the fields to Darkie Hurrell's tar-covered house at the edge of the now dripping and sad-looking woodland. As soon as we opened Darkie's ramshackle wooden gate I could see that something was wrong. The little square house looked bleak and abandoned. The back door, the only one that Darkie ever used, was closed by a chain and a large brass lock.

'Darkie's done a flit,' Father muttered. 'I thought he might.'

'You mean he's gonë?' My Father nodded.

We walked back through the cold, muddy fields. My eyes were flooded with tears. I was filled with bitter pain, but I knew *exactly* what I needed and I wanted it with desperate urgency.

When we reached home I ran to my mother and

whispered to her this secret need. Now I had never really had or needed cuddly toys or teddy bears when I was small. I had ignored a pale blue, woolly version of Wilfred (from the comic strip *Pip, Squeak and Wilfred*) and, since I had grown them, had comforted myself by sniffing the fine hairs on the back of my arm. But now I wanted a doll: a small one, with a pretty face, a blue dress, a bonnet and white shoes.

I begged my mother not to tell my father and I shuddered to think of Uncle Hector's reaction to my request if it should ever come to his knowledge.

When I returned from school the next afternoon there was an exquisite doll, with a blue dress, a bonnet and white shoes, sitting in the corner of the sofa. I took her to my bedroom, examined her minutely, undressed and dressed her and then hid her beneath my pillow. I kept the doll discreetly held beneath the bedclothes that night, until after my father had come to kiss me goodnight.

My mother did not mention or even indirectly refer to my acquisition. After about three weeks or so, I gave my doll to Mother. I had finished with it. I never saw the doll again and never knew what happened to it, for my mother never spoke of it – ever. But I knew that I now had the strength to face life without Darkie Hurrell and, oddly enough, for I don't know why I bothered about him, without Uncle Hector.

I also knew that I had the courage to give Patsy Bailey and Barbara Thorne a thumping when they next tried to bully me. And I did and I got into the devil of a row for it.

6

As 1934 drew to a close, I was struggling to learn to read, and life at Selhurst House School for Girls and Boys was becoming, if not enjoyable, at least tolerable. Christmas that year was magical: with two glorious red boxes containing a troop of the 16th Lancers and a squad of the Middlesex Regiment in scarlet uniforms, a clockwork 4-6-2 Hornby Gauge 0 LMS Standard Locomotive (with track and a tin-plate railway station with the poor passengers flat against the walls) and a Christmas stocking made of white netting, edged with a strip of red crêpe paper, containing a wooden top and whip, some curious unnatural-looking porcelain sailors, a silver paper covered ball (kept intact with white cotton) attached to a length of elastic, a tin model of Sir Malcolm Campbell's racing car *Bluebird*, a card chequerboard with some inadequate wooden draughts, several brazil nuts, sugared almonds and tangerines. The Christmas chicken, which cost *several* shillings, was thrilling, the Christmas pudding quite delicious, the mince pies exquisite, and even the infinitely long speech by King George the Fifth, listened to in solemn silence, on our big wireless set, was bearable.

It was after the King's speech that my mother ventured to wonder what poor Hector was doing at that moment. My father said that he 'didn't care what the silly bugger was doing'. Mother did not reply and the incident passed – driven from my mind, at the time, by the approaching prospect of tea, with fish paste sandwiches, Christmas cake, red jelly and crackers.

49

It was not until I was going to bed that it occurred to me to wonder where Darkie Hurrell was on that golden day. I still vividly remembered his visit to us the previous Christmas when he wore the blue necklace and pinched my mother's mince pies.

'Poor old Darkie,' mused Father, gazing into the fire, 'I hope he's not sleeping too rough tonight.'

I feel shame as I recall my father's concern for the old poacher. Since adolescence I had reduced him to a caricature, an amusing thief and sponger who had very nearly attracted me to his picturesque life of rural crime. This travesty became part of the after-dinner repertoire with which, I now realize, I bored the members of my College. Even worse, there were those jokes with Oakley about how I might have become a successful biologist had I followed my childish inclinations.

Some time in the spring of 1935 my mother received a note from Miss Bunce. It was delivered by the hunch-backed gardener, who was quite transformed by a bowler hat and a dark blue suit. Miss Bunce had, apparently, fallen out with Uncle Hector and intended leaving his employ forthwith.

Without hesitation, my mother donned her coat and dragged me off to catch the bus, *The Queen of the Hills*, to my uncle's village – the first time I had ridden in a country bus. It was a distinctly uncomfortable experience, sitting on wooden slatted seats as the old green bus, with its brass radiator hissing, steadily nosed its way through blossom-filled lanes, to the rising edge of the Wiltshire Downs.

We found Miss Bunce sulking in the cluttered, white-washed scullery, perched uncomfortably on a stool next to the wooden mangle. Uncle Hector was sitting in a wing chair in his dusty library engrossed in an enormous book. I made myself scarce and mooched around the familiar garden, orchard and fields, enjoying the freshness of the vigorously growing grass and spring flowers. I found the smooth white egg of a wood pigeon (then a much less common bird) which I placed carefully in my school cap – to blow when we got home. I also investigated the stack of ancient and curiously carved blocks of stone that I found piled in a grassy corner near the circular pond where my liner had been violated. Evidently, these were the Roman remains from Cricklade that Miss Bunce had told us so excited my uncle. They certainly did not look very impressive. One of them was covered with canvas. I peered underneath to discover a rough carving of a skirted figure with what looked like a dog at its feet. And then I got bored and crept back into the house. I could hear my mother, behind the closed parlour door, giving Uncle Hector a good dressing down. Amazingly, the answers were in apologetic monosyllables.

My uncle walked back with us to the bus stop. He was at his most amiable, and quite devastatingly charming – so tall and distinguished, even in his rough country clothes. On the bus, my mother said that everything was now all right and that Miss Bunce would be staying on as housekeeper. Mother suggested that we should not mention our brief visit to my father. I agreed – there could be trouble in that direction.

It was about the time of the great event of the year, the Silver Jubilee. This, I learned, was to celebrate the twenty-fifth year that George the Fifth had been King. I very much enjoyed such imperial goings on. My father bought a large Union Jack and stuck it on a pole from my bedroom window sill. I could hear the satisfying flapping of the flag as I lay in bed at night. I was also given a blue book full of pictures of the King and Queen and a large scrap-book, again with royal pictures on the cover, into which I inexpertly gummed yet more pictures of royalty with which the newspapers and magazines were filled at the time. There were even celebrations for the children. After a patriotic speech by Miss Daisy (which repeatedly emphasized the extent of the pink on a large map of the world), we all marched off, two by two, scrubbed clean and in our best clothes, each carrying a miniature Union Jack. In a vast crowd of other children we listened to yet another stirring speech and were given a cream-coloured mug with pictures of the King and Queen surrounded by laurel leaves and flags. My mug was given a place of honour in my mother's glass-fronted cabinet, where it joined several older ones commemorating earlier coronations and royal events. From somewhere or other (it might have been Woolworth's, or an official gift) I acquired a very shiny medal, suspended on a gaudy red, white and blue ribbon, showing the head of King George.

I could not help thinking of Uncle Hector at this time. I was sure that he would be enjoying all the flag-waving and was probably contemplating some festive horse-whipping of potential enemies of the Empire. It was, therefore, with some surprise, and very guarded pleasure, that I received a gift that he left especially for me, wrapped in a piece of newspaper, on the bureau in the parlour – another royal mug, cracked, celebrating Queen Victoria's Diamond Jubilee. My mother put it out of sight at the back of her cabinet. I did not mention the gift to my father.

Not many weeks after Uncle Hector's unexpected, damaged gift we again received a call from his house-keeper. She had not come shopping this time, but especially to see my mother. Miss Bunce revealed that she had been saving up for years to visit Canada, to stay for a whole month with a married sister, and to see, for the first time, her niece and nephew. This had seemed an impossible ambition, especially on the wages that she received, but she had inherited a small sum of money and, very surprisingly, Uncle Hector had offered her *twenty pounds*, to help with her expenses. Bunce had arranged for a 'sensible' village woman (Thursa Titcombe) to go up to the house each day to clean, wash and, most importantly, cook Uncle Hector's breakfast and dinner. But Bunce (who showed surprising loyalty, considering the treatment that my uncle had meted out to her) still worried and had come to ask if my mother could, *very* occasionally, keep an eye on these temporary domestic arrangements.

My mother clearly did not want to upset Miss Bunce's carefully laid plans, but there were Father's feelings to think about – he was still smarting from the desecration of his Wellington boot. However, when mother raised the matter with my father, he readily agreed to Bunce's proposal, provided that Mother never actually went near the 'bloody fool'. I was surprised, not only by Father's swearing (in which he now engaged whenever Uncle Hector's name was mentioned) but also by the curious nature of the arrangement that he had approved.

Miss Bunce was driven to Liverpool by Uncle Hector, as we read on a card posted before her ship sailed. And then we heard nothing more of Uncle Hector's domestic arrangements until my mother made a brief morning dash in the *Queen of the Hills* to see for herself, leaving me in charge of Florrie. Her hurried return was marred by a minor disaster which I had precipitated. For a joke, I had locked Florrie in the larder. Unfortunately, I jammed the bolt so firmly home that I could not release it so that our poor maid was trapped, and could only shout horrible threats through the closed door. It took me some time after the furore accompanying Florrie's release by my mother to learn that Uncle Hector was well looked after by Mrs Titcombe and that he claimed it was a much better arrangement than the previous one.

I was, therefore, astonished, one morning several weeks later, to find my uncle's temporary housekeeper vigorously banging away on our impressive brass door knocker (in the shape of a sphinx's head). Thursa Titcombe was a bulky woman, I suppose of middle years. She was very flustered, and sank with obvious relief into half of our big sofa while Florrie went to fetch her a cup of tea. She had come in to town, Thursa gasped, in the 'workman's' (the early morning bus from the village), had hardly slept the previous night, and, what is more, had not been able to look after her kids properly, let alone her husband, Pebbie (all male Titcombes are, or were, called 'Pebbie'), who was very cross about the inadequacies of his supper and breakfast arrangements. Clearly, Uncle Hector had been up to something. I realized that it would be only a matter of time before Thursa exhausted her string of complaints, and told us of the exploits that had precipitated this dramatic visit. I felt a shiver of almost pleasurable apprehension, wondering if he had done something in Thursa's Wellington boot or, perhaps, had been arrested by the police for cruelty to dogs. But it was nothing like that. Uncle Hector was ill.

Thursa eventually told my mother, while Florrie and I hung around listening outside the door (we had been banished at an early stage in the proceedings, presumably in case Uncle Hector really had done something awful),

that her employer had been taken ill the previous afternoon. She had called the doctor, who arrived late in the
evening and had diagnosed pneumonia.

Pneumonia was a serious matter in those days. Father
had once had it. He had become delirious and I vividly
remember listening, again from outside the door, while
he relived appalling experiences at Passchendaele and the
Somme. Once he had mumbled, over and over again:
'Shoot the buggers, Sergeant.' Somehow, I knew that this
meant shooting German prisoners, for my father was an
artillery officer and it didn't sound to me like an order to
fire one of those huge guns that he had showed me so
often in faded, sepia photographs. This became one of
the many things that I worried about at the time and I
often imagined a row of grey, bloodstained, figures lying
in the mud, their spiked helments still on their heads,
with my father standing over them, in service dress,
wearing his Sam Browne belt.

My mother acted very quickly when she heard Thursa
Titcombe's news. She collected together some clothes,
put them in the smallest of our battered leather suitcases
and departed with Thursa on the returning *Queen of the
Hills*. I was left with Florrie and a message to give to my
father asking him to drive out later in the day to Uncle
Hector's house.

Mother answered the door when we arrived in the
Austin after tea. She came out and walked up and down
the lavender-bordered brick path with my father who, to
my relief, was not at all angry at her errand of mercy. I
disappeared to talk to the two dogs who, I hoped, would
be spared their customary savage discipline – at least for
a while.

I came running back from behind the elder hedge

55

anxious to hear what had been decided. My father was to take me home while my mother stayed on to look after Uncle Hector. I certainly did not *want* to be parted from her and probably wept, though I cannot be sure of this. There was also the worry that *she* would catch pneumonia.

As we drove back, my father mentioned another, bitterly disappointing, complication. In only ten days' time, my mother and I were to have had a seaside holiday with my proper uncle, my mother's brother, and my Auntie Nell, at that gloriously exciting place: Sand Bay. My Uncle David had bought an acre or so of sandy marram grass on a southern shore of the Bristol Channel and had erected on it an ex-Army, wooden bungalow, for a holiday home. I used to dream of Sand Bay, of the great expanse of glistening mud at low tide, the excitement of being with Uncle David who always contrived interesting things for me, of the calls of seagulls and of the uniquely exciting wooden bungalow which smelt of wood polish and paraffin.

While we were at Sand Bay, my father had planned to go on a fishing trip to Scotland with Sid Thorpe (another victim of Uncle Hector). I knew that my father had been very excited by this projected adventure which was now also threatened by Uncle Hector's inconsiderate attack of pneumonia. There was one thing that I was certain about: I would *not* go by myself with my aunt and uncle to Sand Bay, despite all the much dreamt-of delights of that glorious place. Yet I did not want to wreck my father's Scottish adventure, the planning of which I had vicariously enjoyed.

The difficulties were resolved by my decision – the first major one that I ever made. I would join my mother at Uncle Hector's, so that Father could go off with Sid Thorpe to Scotland. Such a noble offer, I thought, would certain rate a pretty impressive present from Scotland on my father's return. I knew what I wanted: a Scottish dirk, that I could stick in the top of my socks.

Father seemed very grateful for my apparent generosity and not as worried as I had expected at the prospect of his wife and son living under the roof of the violator of his Wellington boot.

I was rather apprehensive – in fact, not a little frightened at the thought of living in close proximity to Uncle Hector once again. However, I comforted myself with the thought that he might still be very ill, could perhaps die, or at the very worst, only recover to such a limited extent that he would be incapable of serious dog beating.

7

I was disappointed in the hoped-for debilitation of Uncle Hector. I realized this, immediately after being deposited at his front door with my suitcase and a few carefully chosen (British) toys. Uncle Hector emerged from the parlour, a place he rarely frequented in Miss Bunce's regime, and radiated good humour. He only seemed somewhat paler than usual.

Now I had devised an overall plan which I believed would help me cope with the difficult situation that I would face in my uncle's house. I had decided, first, to employ youthful charm against my formidable host. This strategy was not entirely based on conceit, because I knew, from close observation, that it could be most effective. The trouble was that it really only succeeded with elderly, middle-class ladies. However, given my very limited resources, and very difficult position, I felt that it might have some marginal value in future relations with my extraordinary uncle. Secondly, I had determined that I would minimize direct confrontations. I would simply make myself scarce.

Looking back, I now realize that Uncle Hector adopted similar tactics. Whenever we encountered each other, he had some kind words for me, but most of the time he kept to his own preserves and I only saw him at meal times and when chatting with my mother in the parlour.

Mother was strangely transformed. She obviously got on very well with Thursa, whom she described as a good worker. At times she was positively skittish, especially when she was engaged in what she called 'pulling Uncle Hector's leg', largely about his strange hobby. She sometimes wore Darkie Hurrell's Roman brooch and Uncle never could find out how she had come by it. Oddly, she seemed not to worry unduly about what I was up to. Before, when we were at Uncle Hector's, she would regularly seek me out to make sure that I was not in any kind of danger or, worse, 'mischief'. I assumed, very reasonably, that my mother had, at last, recognized, my advancing years and was, thus, treating me in a much less babyish way. Whatever the reasons for my new-found freedom, it suited my second strategy very well indeed.

To assist this and because it was enjoyable in its own right, I set out to establish a secret hideout. After some preliminary scouting, I hit on the idea of making my clandestine headquarters at the top of the field which ran steeply up from the vegetable garden at the back of the house. This site had two useful attributes. First, an approach could be made with maximum secrecy. On the right-hand side of the field was a long, hollow hedge (it was not until quite recently that I learned that this represented a Saxon boundary, the track between two land holdings that had become hedged over). The advantage of this hedge was that it provided an unseen route which enabled me to walk off in the general direction of the land behind the mushroom-supported barn, and then to dive through a hole in the hollow hedge and proceed, at right angles, in the leafy gloom up to the top of the field. My lair was also situated in a hedge, the one bordering my uncle's property at the highest point of the same field. I had chosen a particularly thorny part of this hedge in which there was a very useful tree, which I could easily climb. This afforded a useful vantage point, not only to view my uncle's land, but also to spy into the lane which ran along the other side of the hedge.

To build my lair, I committed some petty larceny of what I imagined would be little-valued tools and potential building materials that were scattered in abundance all around my uncle's strange little kingdom.

My most useful acquisition was a rusty, rather blunt axe which I found in the barn. I purloined some one-inch nails, a large hammer, a length of rope and several bits of wire. I also earmarked four sheep hurdles (purchased for, but not incorporated in, my uncle's device on top of the front wall), which I discovered in some stinging nettles near the pond, and several old sacks that I found under miscellaneous junk near the fearsome looking man-trap.

Bit by bit, I transported the building materials up the hollow hedge to the top of the steep field. I had to act with considerable secrecy, to avoid not only my uncle and mother, but also Thursa Titcombe and the hump-backed gardener. But I was very cunning, or at least I thought so. I certainly spent a great deal of time checking up on the whereabouts of everybody, before attempting transportation of any of the major items. The sheep hurdles were the most difficult. They were awkward, very heavy indeed and, as they completely obscured me, were most likely to be spotted, presumably moving of their own volition across open ground between the end of the elder hedge and the wooden barn on mushrooms. However, I got them up to the barn and into the hollow hedge late in the afternoon, after Thursa had left, while Uncle Hector and my mother were talking with the gardener in the courtyard behind the house. It was then only a matter of humping the hurdles along the shaded green tunnel to the top corner of the field.

I remember the deep feeling of satisfaction after I had

collected together the items that I required, even though I was very tired and was severely scolded by my mother for a tear in my trousers and the dirty state of my blouse. To my surprise, and real gratitude, Uncle Hector took my side, saying that I was not a 'namby-pamby' and was turning into a real boy.

I looked forward that night to resting in the little room at the end of the corridor, but was extremely embarrassed, and outraged, when Mother brought my uncle up to say goodnight – just as I was getting undressed. I was very relieved that I was at least putting on my striped flannel pyjamas and not the girlish night-gown that I had until recently still been forced to wear. I was also relieved that I had hidden, under the bed, the hated combinations which I had failed to persuade my mother were so cissy.

The next morning, I ate my breakfast with alacrity, slimy bits of egg white and all, and was off up the hollow hedge to the site of my proposed hideout. I had great plans for a sort of tree-hut or a big-game hunter's plat-form, to be constructed with the aid of the sheep hurdles, rope and bits of wire. But my plans turned out to be difficult, if not downright impossible. My chief difficulty was that the branches of the tree did not provide any-where that I could lay one of the sheep hurdles to form the platform. In the end, I compromised by using the hurdles to make a simple hut on the ground near the back of the boundary hedge, so that it would certainly not be seen from my uncle's field. I tried to rope the hurdles together, cutting the strands with great difficulty using the rusty axe. But in the end I had a small crazy-looking structure, with the roof and three sides formed from the hurdles. The open end I closed off by hanging one of the sacks.

As I stood back to look at my handiwork, I had to admit that my little hut was pathetic. I became so depressed that I flung down the axe, slouched off down the hedge tunnel, and did not return to the scene of which I had had such high hopes until the end of the afternoon. This visit confirmed the failure of my project. The industrious chirruping of a grasshopper seemed to mock my incompetence.

I now felt totally vulnerable and without refuge. The sagging structure that I had attempted with such enthusiasm could clearly not provide the protection I so desperately needed in the uncertainty of the days that lay ahead. I was swept with feelings of guilt at living in the house of someone who had humiliated my father. Worse, I began to wonder how Mother could be so obviously and disloyally enjoying her stay here, especially as we could have been at Sand Bay together in total happiness.

Supper that night was a dismal affair. I crept off to bed early and pretended to be asleep when my mother came to my room to say goodnight.

The next morning, breakfast passed without incident (despite my uncle's obvious irritation at my rejection of fat streaky bacon). Afterwards I wandered out into the misty morning of what promised to be another hot day. I could hardly bear to think of my ramshackle hut, which was such a poor substitute for my grandiose scheme for a big-game hunter's platform or a treehouse. However, there seemed no other place for me. So I walked slowly around the mushroom barn, into the hedge and along its green interior towards the scene of my childish failure of the previous day.

When I reached the top of my secret highway, I received the biggest shock of my life. Unbelievably, the inadequate, crazy structure, that I had abandoned so ignominiously, had been transformed. The sheep hurdles were now part of something that looked like a little house. They formed a roof, with sloping sides, supported by stout lengths of wood which had been dug into the ground. A piece of green canvas had been neatly tied over the roof hurdles so that it would even keep out rain. The walls were made of the sacks. I could see that these could be rolled up to leave the sides open, which would be a great advantage in the summer heat. There was even a rope hanging down beside the trunk of the tree so that I could climb up to the leafy branches to spy out the land.

I was overjoyed and then apprehensive. Who had done this wonderful thing? Could it have been Uncle Hector? He would have had to have done it at night. It would hardly have been the hump-backed gardener. My mother could never have built such a thing. Perhaps it was a trap, set by my uncle to catch me as the man-trap would snap shut in the orchard grass. If I thanked him, he would know who had tried to build the house at the top of his field. Perhaps he was trying to be nice to me so as to get me on his side and away from my father. I did not like either possibility and fled without further ado.

I spent most of the rest of the morning trying to make a toy raft out of straight twigs. I attempted to tie them together with some string, which I obtained, quite legally, from Mrs Titcombe. It was not a success and, even if it had been, I could not think how I could make a mast and a sail for it.

After lunch, while the others were sitting in the parlour and the hump-back was eating bread and awful-looking fat bacon in the shade of a hedge, I ran to the top of the steep field by the now familiar route. The transformed house was still there. I had not imagined it. Again, I panicked and ran back into the orchard. I lay in the long grass listening to the summer hum, watching insects crawl up the stems and small birds flit from branch to branch overhead. Then I must have dozed, for it was later in the afternoon when I again became conscious of the orchard scents and sounds arounds me.

My first thoughts were of the hurdle house and, still drowsy, I stumbled uphill in the leafy cool of the hollow hedge for one more look. Nothing had changed. The magnificent structure stood in the shaded light. The rope hung invitingly from the branch.

Then, with a thrill of apprehension, I saw, lying in the opening in the sacking that served as a door, the bright blue wrapping of an unopened halfpenny bar of chocolate. I walked over, and picked it up. Only my mother would know of my greed for this particular brand.

'Hello, Master James.'

The low voice was unforgettably familiar. Darkie Hurrell. And there he was standing by the tree looking down and enjoying my astonishment.

'It was *you* that built the hut!'

'That's right, young 'un. You'd made a middlin' bad job of it.'

I wanted to hug Darkie, but knew that I couldn't. What ever would he have thought?

'Did you leave the chocolate?'

'I did, Master James. I knowed which you like.'

I knew what my father would have said in the circumstances. He would have said: 'Well I'm damned.' I would have liked to say that, but I knew it wouldn't come out right, so I contented myself with a single 'Gosh'.

We both sat down in front of the hurdle hut, which was now *really* mine. I broke the chocolate in two and gave

Darkie the bigger bit. I knew that he was always hungry. It went down in one gulp.

Then I looked more closely at him. He was not the smart Darkie that I had known at home. He looked tired, his clothes were dusty and torn and his fingernails, which had always been clean, were black along the tops.

'You know I done a flit?'

'Yes, my father said, We came to see you but you were gone.'

Darkie explained that life had become difficult for him in his little house by the wood. He couldn't pay his rent and had been nearly caught on three nights running. Caught? What did he mean? Then, in a single flash, I realized that Darkie Hurrell was what Uncle Hector swore about: a poacher. Not that I minded. If Darkie was one, then poachers were good, although I worried a little about the killing. Anyhow, Darkie had to be exactly the opposite of Uncle Hector. I knew that Darkie would not want to horse-whip anyone, would certainly not have peed in my father's Wellington and would definitely not have flung one of my toys in the stinging nettles.

A second, appalling, thought grew. Darkie was in great danger, for if Uncle Hector caught him then anything might happen. Darkie laughed again at my quixotic change of mood.

'Don't worry, little 'un. He won't catch me. I keep moving along and sleeping rough.'

This was consoling, and showed professional confidence, but was not wholly convincing. I knew more than most people about Uncle Hector. Darkie tried to comfort me again.

'*Don't worry*. Anyway, they all say round here that

he's daft. The place is full of Roman remains, skeletons and such like.'

So that was it. Uncle Hector really was mad. It explained a lot. I knew now that I had to be very careful and that only my mother could control my Uncle Hector.

8

Like so many things in my life at that time, a simple pleasure such as the reappearance of Darkie Hurrell was flawed by worries about his safety. My first concern was to provide sustenance for my old·friend. Darkie had no objections to this, although he emphasized the need for caution.

'Things here are not like they are in your home, Master James, so don't get stripping the larder.'

I though that my mother would have seen the funny side of that piece of advice.

My home now seemed very far away and I wondered if Florrie and the neighbours were looking after Sandy and Jack properly.

Darkie said that the best thing to do would be to bring food as late as possible in the afternoon. My little hut was a good place for us to meet, because he could easily push through the hedge from the lane and leave by the same route. We also had a clear view of the field and the entrance from the vegetable garden at the back of the house. He could also then move on, to ply his trade, after I had gone in for my supper.

I decided to use two main sources of food for Darkie. I would discreetly cull from the vegetable garden and, at greater risk, would take a levy from the larder next to the scullery. Both of these sources could be most easily raided in the afternoon. Fortunately, there were some raspberries left and young carrots that could be pulled without leaving obvious gaps in the rows. I also took a few plums, but they seemed hard and very sour when I bit into them.

My technique in the larder was essentially the same as that in the vegetable garden. Thursa Titcombe always left by mid-afternoon so that as long as I knew where my mother and Uncle Hector were, then all was well. I decided on a general attrition rather than outright theft of large items. So I would cut a slice from a lardy cake or a loaf of bread, hack off a lump of cheese, take a handful of raisins, stuff some biscuits in my pockets, and lift a pickled onion or two (Darkie was especially fond of these).

Before our next meeting, I laid out my haul of food-stuffs on an old sheet of newspaper for Darkie. He was delighted and tucked in vigorously. He had a bottle of beer in his pocket. I sat back enjoying a most pleasant feeling of proprietorship as my friend ate his way steadily through an astonishing assortment of victuals.

After his meal, Darkie relaxed with his back against the trunk of the tree and his long legs stuck out straight. We had so many things to talk about. But first I wanted to know how he had found my hideout and known that the hurdle hut was mine.

'That was easy: I seen you arrive. I was in the field opposite, when your dad drove you past. I found this here, because it's on my way into your uncle's place.'

It seemed that Darkie had not been long in the neighbourhood. He had moved into the area only a few days before I arrived and would shift on again fairly soon. Darkie explained that he did not settle anywhere for too long. That way he did not attract the undue attention of gamekeepers, farmers or rival poachers. He said that he knew how to make himself comfortable. Often he did casual work for farmers and later in the summer might

68

help with the harvest. This way he made a little money so that he could 'put up' in the worst of the winter weather. He had evidently also charmed a vicar and his wife, in a village some ten miles away, rather as he had my family. They also allowed him occasionally to sleep inside when the weather became very wet or exceptionally cold.

Darkie told me that Uncle Hector's place was ideal for his purposes. My uncle was 'light-headed in all his limbs' (a curious phrase that I assumed referred to his supposed madness) and certainly did not know anything about preserving his game. According to Darkie, the place was stuffed with pheasants, partridges, hares and rabbits, largely due to my uncle's lack of interest in shooting or agriculture. At that time of the year Darkie largely confined himself to rabbiting, for which, he considered, my uncle should be grateful to him.

Darkie told me that he had got rid of his gun. He looked away when he told me this and I knew that it hurt him to speak about it. Now he hunted mostly with snares (for rabbits) and rat-traps (for the occasional pheasant). He could still tickle a trout, and later on would pick downland blackberries (better than any other, Darkie said), and sloes, hunt for mushrooms and blewits (blue-stems) and fill his pockets with hazelnuts from tall lonely hedges.

Now that I was older, I could better appreciate his marvellous knowledge of the animals and plants of the Wiltshire countryside. Darkie always had something inter-esting to tell: of stone curlews, strange birds with knobbly knees and huge yellow eyes, like a cat's, that foraged at twilight and filled the chalky valleys with their eerie calls; and of the great bustard, which Darkie said was like an enormous stone curlew, weighing pounds, that had once lived up on the Downs.

Darkie knew a lot about plants. He would talk about strange ones: frog and bee orchids, twayblade, bird's-nest orchids. I always remembered what he told me, even very difficult names, like squinancy-wort. Mother could never discover how I knew that beautiful little flower.

He knew stories about really interesting people, like old Eli Winters, the last man in Wiltshire to get dogs to dig up truffles. It was years before I realized that they were not that particularly delicious kind of chocolate. Darkie also told me about Wayland Smith's Cave near the Ridgeway where he used to rest up and occasionally cook a rabbit for his supper. The smoke couldn't be seen among the trees that surrounded the cave. Long ago, Darkie said, the Wayland Smith was supposed to have lived in the cave and magically shod horses. If the horse was left, with one farthing placed on a particular stone, then within one hour, or overnight (I forget which), the horse would be found with a brand-new set of shoes and the farthing would be gone.

I was not particularly impressed by the story of Wayland Smith, but vividly imagined Darkie sitting at the entrance to something the size of Fingal's Cave, cooking his rabbit. Such was the magic of that circle of trees and the strange piled stones, that I was not disappointed by the reality when I persuaded my father to drive there, shortly afterwards.

Darkie Hurrell also told of a writer who once lived nearby. Apparently Uncle David, with typical kindness and wit, had given Darkie two books (as I later realized: *The Amateur Poacher* and *The Gamekeeper at Home*). The books had been lost in the flit from the little tarred cottage. They had been very precious to Darkie. The writer was a strange chap who had lived not far away, at Coate, where he had been known as 'Daftie' Jefferies.

70

But Darkie Hurrell had loved those books for their knowledge of his countryside. He wished that he had them to show me. I remember wondering if it was only daft people who did interesting things, like writing such books. Perhaps that was why Uncle Hector was so peculiar. As Darkie had just told me, the village people called him 'daft'.

Uncle was, in fact, contemplating, at that very time, a project which would certainly have been so categorized by most of his neighbours. He revealed his scheme to me one morning just after Darkie Hurrell's arrival on the scene. I listened with embarrassed, but growing, interest. I was even more apprehensive of Uncle Hector now that I was harbouring one of his proclaimed enemies, but, nevertheless, I could not resist a feeling of rising excitement as he outlined his latest scheme. What he was planning was to put together the pile of curiously carved Roman stones that Miss Bunce had first told us about. They were at that moment looking neglected, partly obscured by a vigorous growth of weeds, but my uncle told me that they were very special. He said that they were part of what had been a Roman temple; the canvas-covered one was the altar.

My uncle had discovered them while poking about in an old house which was being demolished. By rights, the find should have been reported, in which case these glorious objects would have ended up in a museum. Uncle Hector had no intention of allowing that to happen. He therefore got the workmen to remove what he wanted from the rubble, hired a lorry and brought back his archaeological trophies in some triumph and great secrecy. The next stage of the operation was about to commence. This involved the clearing out of part of one of the flint buildings and the re-creation of the Roman altar. Only when this was completed would he announce his find to the world and challenge any 'damn busybodies' to take it from him. I strongly suspected that it was this aspect of the operation which primarily attracted him. I could just imagine him hurling defiance at, or manhandling, whatever forces were routinely marshalled for the recovery of ancient Roman stones in the mid-1930s.

I must admit that, despite very severe reservations about Uncle Hector, I too was greatly attracted by this aspect of the affair. I quickly indulged in a new variant of a familiar fantasy: I was a defender in an exciting siege in which I would distinguish myself by some minor act of heroism and, at a stroke, re-establish myself in my uncle's eyes as a true patriot. And then the dream faded as I remembered my loyalties, especially to my absent father, who at that very moment was probably wading in some Scottish river in defiled Wellington boots.

There were also strictly practical considerations. It occurred to me that it would be best if I co-operated with my uncle, as he seemed to want. If I did, it would at least keep him away from the top of the steep field and, presumably, in a relatively good mood. The main difficulty would be the purloining of food for Darkie and, of course, our late afternoon meetings. A less, but still daunting, problem would be that of maintaining good relations, for I still shrank from my Uncle Hector. I could not understand him even though I was fascinated by practically everything that he did.

My uncle did not start work on his project that day. He lounged around drinking tea with my mother who came down very late for breakfast. Then he cornered me as I was passing by on some trivial errand. Without preamble, he announced that we were going for a drive, and marched me off to the 'bull-nose'.

His abrupt action filled me with alarm. Was he planning to abandon me, miles from anywhere, in the midst of the Downs? There was no telling what might happen and I boarded the car with considerable trepidation. However, with beech trees, tall hedgerows and then open, rolling downland whizzing past the long grey bonnet, my alarm subsided, for Uncle Hector was talking and talking. I strained to listen to his husky voice, now urgent, compelling and not the least bit cross, above the engine noise and the rushing air. To my intense surprise, I realized that my uncle was talking of ancient times: about the massive earthworks, silhouetted against the downland sky line, of the grey wethers (the sandstone boulders, or sarsen stones, scattered like flocks of sheep on the chalky hills), and of the grassy tombs of ancient warriors, of the great turf highway, the Ridgeway, which once carried the trade from half a continent.

Car journeys usually seemed interminable, but this one passed almost without notice. We halted near a huge green hill, like a gigantic pudding basin on the side of the flinty road.

'Silbury,' Uncle Hector announced.

My uncle evidently did not intend that we should get out of the car and, as I would have liked, run up the exciting great hill. Silbury had been built by man, thousands of years before. No one knew why, or what for, but my uncle said that he had the secret. Although bursting with curiosity, I did not ask what it was and my uncle spoke no more of that strange early pyramid as we drove on.

I did not look at my Uncle Hector as he talked and talked on that distant summer day. He was still the man my father refused to meet, who might hunt Darkie Hurrell and who would probably hurt me again in unexpected ways.

We must have looked an odd pair as we climbed from the 1926 Morris at Avebury, nearly fifty years ago. A tall, distinguished-looking man, dressed like a workman, in battered corduroys and an old tweed jacket. Trotting, deliberately a pace behind, a solemn little boy, in a large grey felt hat, trying unsuccessfully to suppress his excitement and not to skip with pleasure on the springy downland turf.

Around us were huge, grey stones set on end, like petrified giants. We walked right round the great stone circle, my uncle all the time telling me of the people who had built this magic place.

I think I understood, even then, that my interests would be those of the two strange men who had chosen to reveal themselves to me. Those interests, I now realize, were part of the sequence which led to my bird-watching, to my sixteenth-century studies and, inexorably, to the obnoxious De Freville.

The memory of that dreadful undergraduate caused me to groan into the darkness as I lay at Molly's side, tired after my day on the salt marshes, but unable to sleep. Molly stirred at the sound and mumbled. I waited in the darkness for sleep to reclaim her. Inexplicably the bedroom smelt of fresh oil paint. What on earth was I going to say to the Senior Tutor about the request that De Freville had made to change his History supervisor? I didn't believe that he really wanted to. He derived too much sadistic pleasure from harrying me on the finer points of Lollardy and my complete inability to prove that the Black Death had any effect whatever on the growth of heresy. And to think that it was I who had

74

been so insistent that he should be admitted to the College, despite a rather unimpressive showing in the entrance examination.

An owl screeched just outside the bedroom window. Funny that it should have become a typical suburban night sound. What would Darkie have thought of that short-eared owl on the marshes? I shut my eyes and became once more an earnest little boy worried about the safety of my strange friend.

9

It was difficult to collect Darkie's rations that afternoon because Thursa stayed on to clean up after our delayed meal. But I tugged up some onions and carrots from the hump-back's garden, and cut a hunk of bread and stole a lump of cheese as soon as Thursa left.

Darkie was waiting for me when I ran up the hollow hedge and burst into our meeting place. I was still excited by my trip to Avebury and gabbled away about it to him.

He had found some tiny wild strawberries and had picked some watercress. I had not known until then that strawberries grew wild, but found them quite delicious. Although Darkie had brought them especially for me, I only ate a few, so as to leave as many as possible for him. I was not keen on the cress.

My friend said that he'd had a good bag on the previous night and sold most of it to a man in the village where he had picked the watercress. The man's wife had given him a piece of pie and some lardy cake. He had bought some tobacco, a bottle of beer and, also, an earthenware bottle of ginger beer for me. He lit his pipe and, rather like my uncle earlier in the day, began to talk without apparently expecting any responses from me.

Darkie told me that he had been born in London, sonewhere in the East End; a very rough place by his account. His mother had been a gipsy.

'What you would call a Diddycoy, Master James, but you'd be wrong, though.'

His mother had, apparently, run away from her father,

a navvy, who had taken her to London. Soon after Darkie was born, his father had left (done a 'flit', I supposed). His mother had eventually gone off with another man, sending Darkie to live with his father's mother in a village on the other side of my town. He had hated the village school (where there was much reciting of tables and canings) and had left at the earliest opportunity to work in a factory. He had disliked that as well and, when his grandmother died, had taken to doing odd jobs and then more and more poaching. He had liked his tarred house, and his garden, but still preferred his present life to one spent as a factory- or farm-hand.

Soon he would be moving on. It was not safe to stay for long in the same place and he knew were he might be quite comfortable when the weather grew colder. I felt, almost simultaneously, a surge of loneliness as Darkie spoke of leaving, relief that he would be safe from my uncle and some pleasure that he would still be close by for a couple more days or so.

At supper Uncle Hector returned to his scheme for the Roman altar. We would start to prepare the coach house the next morning. I was to be his assistant. I could see that my mother was pleased at this, but I felt uncertain and guilty at the prospect.

That evening as my mother came to bid me goodnight she brought a postcard from my father. It had tactfully been put into an envelope, for which I was grateful because it showed a picture of Bonzo (a favourite children's cartoon character of the time) dressed in a Highland costume. As I looked at the picture of the ridiculous dog, in kilt and bonnet, I felt that my chances of a Scottish dirk must be remote. However, I was very pleased to hear that my father would be returning within a few days to take me back to home, dog and jackdaw.

I awoke abruptly the next morning, before the familiar dawn chorus, with only a glimmer of light filtering through the little window. Shortly after, I heard a distant door close. The light grew stronger. Some time later a door was closed again. Then I knew that something was very wrong, for my uncle's voice became clearly audible. He was obviously in a great temper and was raging away to himself. His shouting had roused my mother and we both crept along the corridor in our dressing gowns. I caught the word 'poacher'.

I walked downstairs behind my mother, sick with apprehension. In the hall stood Uncle Hector, his shirt tail hanging and boots unlaced. With some difficulty we learned that he had been awoken by the sound of a single shot. Then he had heard a second, he believed from the direction of the orchard. After hastily dressing, he had run into the early dawn light, clutching his dog-beating cudgel, only to find a scattering of pigeon feathers at the far side of the orchard. No one was in sight.

The thought that his neighbours might view his chimney pots had nearly driven Uncle Hector frantic; the knowledge that a poacher had trespassed and shot a bird on my uncle's land produced a truly spectacular effect. Everything else was forgotten. The estate was to be made poacher-proof and, if not, then this vermin was to be eliminated when it penetrated my uncle's defences.

I was by now sure that the poacher could not have been Darkie Hurrell. He did not have a gun and, in any case, had always impressed on me the simple efficiency of the snare and rat-trap. However, we would obviously have to be careful and I was pleased that both Darkie and I would soon be leaving this dreadful place, which only yesterday had been excitingly transformed by my uncle's charm and interest.

I was very surprised when I realized that my mother was not particularly upset by my uncle's latest display. She smiled at me and suggested that we should prepare for our breakfast, which she would cook as it was still far too early an hour for Mrs Titcombe.

Uncle Hector now lost all interest in his Roman project. We were on a war footing and he knew what he was going to do. First, with the aid of the hump-back he was going to do his best to make his frontier impregnable. He would get barbed wire that very day. Secondly, he would set the trap.

Even at the age of six, or thereabouts, I could hardly believe what I heard. My mother laughed, but I was appalled. I could not bear to think of an animal with its foot caught in a steel trap, let alone a man.

My uncle spent the rest of the morning on his anti-poaching precautions. At about noon I heard him calling for me as I sat under the mushroom barn, whittling a stick and worrying whether I would have the courage to see Darkie Hurrell that afternoon and steal his food for him.

'Come here, boy.' He never called me by my name. He was so different from Darkie Hurrell who inserted 'James' into every other sentence of his conversations with me.

He motioned for me to follow him into the orchard. Right in the middle, where a rough path ran between two large apple trees, he stopped, and, with his stick, pushed some tall grass to one side, and then let it fall back again.

'Don't go near that, unless you want your foot caught.'

I was standing in fright, and could not see what was hidden in the grass.

'And don't tell you mother, if you want to keep in my good books.'

79

So saying, my uncle took the stick that I had been whittling and stuck it in the ground. He broke a branch from the tree and, with his own knife, stripped off the bark and thrust the glistening white stick into the ground – about three feet from the other one.

'Now we will know where it is.'

It would have been the only way, because the grass had fallen back into position and looked like any other in that great orchard.

I did not speak, but ran straight back to my mother. She was in her bedroom, tidying up and folding some clothes into the drawer of a dressing table. I whispered to her what I had seen, but begged her not to tell my uncle that I had spoken to her about it. She laughed at my fear and told me that of course my uncle would not set a man-trap. Had I seen it? Then I should not be silly and, furthermore, if I was going to frighten myself in this way I had better not go into the orchard at all.

After lunch, my uncle cornered me again. He too ordered me to keep out of the orchard.

I was now desperately worried about the meeting with Darkie Hurrell later in the afternoon and shrank from the prospect of stealing food at such a dangerous time. Then I hit on a good idea: I would ask for my pocket money. I had not had any for weeks and I estimated that there must be ninepence due to me. With this money I could buy food for Darkie. This should not be difficult. Only a day or so before I had been shopping, for the first time ever. Mrs Titcombe had run out of cheese (the poor lady just could not understand *where* it was going) and had asked me to walk down to the village shop to buy more.

I collected my overdue pocket money, made up to

tenpence by my mother, and departed through the hole in the hedge, which was my front entrance owing to my inability to operate the heavy latch on the wall door. I felt quite important with so much money in my pocket, going off to buy provisions for a grown-up and, if I had any money left, some confectionery for myself. As I walked down the steep road to the little thatched shop, I decided that baked beans would be ideal for Darkie. They were certainly one of my favourite foods and I enjoyed them cold, if I ever got the chance to eat them that way. I would use what money was left over to get some sherbet fountains for myself. I particularly liked the liquorice pipes, stuck into yellow tubes to suck up the delightful fizzy powder and, also, for subsequent consumption when the sherbet was finished.

As I walked back I realized that a tin of baked beans would be a conspicuous item which would certainly excite adult enquiries. So I did not return by the same route, but continued up the hill, turning right, at the top, into the dusty lane which bordered the hedge that incorporated my hideout. I popped the tin down a convenient rabbit hole in the hedge bottom, continued along the lane a little further, and dived into the hedge, using Darkie Hurrell's entrance.

Having checked that the hurdle house was still safe I crept down the hollow hedge and emerged behind the barn, to startle my strolling mother by my abrupt appearance at the centre of my uncle's estate.

I spent the rest of the afternoon sucking sherbet through the liquorice pipes, talking to the tethered dogs, trying, unsuccessfully, to make rude noises with blades of grass held between the edges of my thumbs and making regular forays into the house to read, with some difficulty, the time on my uncle's grandfather clock.

At the appointed time, I was waiting, not in the usual place, but out in the lane, concealed among tall grass. Darkie soon appeared walking without any of the scrunching noises that would have been made by lesser mortals. Although I did not move, he spotted me and chuckled.

'What are you doing out here, then? Have they chucked you out?'

I ignored his sally and burst out with the awful news of the early morning incident and, particularly, of my uncle's terrible rage. Darkie was certainly very interested, but not in the least perturbed.

'Just one of the village cowboys. I don't suppose that you uncle will manage to catch him.'

But that was not all, I insisted. There was the trap that had been set in the orchard. It was a terrible thing and would break a man's leg. It was set in long grass and was marked with two white sticks that were stuck in the ground on either side of it. Like my mother, Darkie was amused by my concern.

'I don't think that even your precious uncle would put out a man-trap. Not in 1935 he wouldn't.'

Then the same question as my mother. Had I seen it? Again I had to admit that I had not. Well, not exactly. But I knew it was there. I had seen it on the wall of the coach house and there were the two white sticks.

'But you didn't see it in the grass, Master James. Did you? Your uncle has a lot of queer things hanging on his walls and he don't put them out in his orchard, does he? He's just having you on.'

And that was that as far as Darkie was concerned. It was as though he just would not believe that anyone would be so dementedly unprofessional as to seek such a means of dealing with a man of his gentlemanly calling. 'Not in 1935!'

I could not see what the date had to do with it. If someone was going to set a man-trap, then they were going to set one – irrespective of the date. But I supposed that Darkie was right and produced the tin of baked beans. The tall quiet man was amused by the offering. He said that he would not eat them there; he would warm them up later on.

He sat chatting by the side of the quiet little lane. I told Darkie that I would be off soon and how much I was looking forward to seeing Jack again. He said that he would be moving on too, but would try to leave something for my collection before he went.

So we said goodbye until tomorrow, and I watched as my strange, lonely companion walked back the way he had come and, without a backward glance, slipped out of sight in his unique, mysterious way.

After he had gone, all my doubts returned. If the trap was not set, then why had my uncle told me to keep out of the orchard? And whatever Mother said, my uncle was, at least to me, dangerous.

As I walked down the secret leafy tunnel I had an idea. I would see if the man-trap was still on the wall in the coach house. I pulled open the door and saw just the rusty nail on which the terrible device had been suspended. So it had been taken down. But then I realized that this was the place that was to be cleared out for the Roman altar. I could see that other things had already been moved. Again there was no certainty, so I gave up and walked slowly back for my supper, which I suspected would be a considerable ordeal with my uncle in his present terrible mood.

10

Next morning, I struggled into consciousness to the distant sound of my uncle's voice. Once again he was raging, with the same effect as before: my mother and I crept down the panelled staircase in our dressing gowns to encounter Uncle Hector – fully dressed and consumed by a gigantic rage. Even in my fright, I was fascinated by the tiny bulging blue veins at his temple, by his contorted face and the sheer volume of his voice.

'Swine,' he bellowed. 'Bloody swine.'

He was brandishing a rat-trap, sprung, with a single baked bean impaled on a wire spike.

'And living on my land,' he stuttered. 'With my hurdles and using *my* tools.'

My mother was not amused that morning. She pushed him by the arm into the parlour and shut the door in my face. I remained, transfixed and yet conscious that my hands were shaking. And then the door was torn open. I stood directly facing the wild, incoherent figure in which, strangely, I sensed a great loneliness.

'Did you build that thing in the top meadow?' Before I could say anything, 'No. How could you? The canvas was stolen from somewhere else.'

My mother shut the door again and gradually my uncle's voice quietened to a husky stream of hate. He would stay up all night; he would be there in the morning; he would beat the swine. And then I fled, across the hall, up the thrice-turning stairs, along the corridor still rosy in the early light, to the familiar little room and bitter grief.

Breakfast was late that morning and, to my relief, Uncle Hector was not present. I was grateful for the reassuring presence of Mrs Titcombe. I lingered in the sunny parlour. There was nowhere I could go.

The hurdle house had been a sanctuary. I had hardly used it, but the knowledge of it had given me security and strength. And now it was destroyed. I knew that it would have been thrown down. Darkie and I would never meet there again. My only comfort was the thought that he was safe and the only thing that I could do now was somehow to stop him trying to come to our broken hideout and certain discovery by my uncle.

Clearly my mother was concerned that I might have been frightened by Uncle Hector's latest outburst. She spent the rest of the morning with me, reading aloud, playing Snap and Ludo. I was grateful for her love, which I needed desperately. She was wearing the Roman brooch that Darkie had given her. I wondered whether I dare tell her about him, but decided against it. You could never tell with grown-ups.

After lunch, my mother produced some drawing paper and my crayons and suggested that I should do a nice drawing for Mrs Titcombe. I cannot remember what I drew, but it was probably a row of battleships (a favourite theme) spitting orange crayoned flames from their guns and belching clouds of scribbled black smoke from their funnels.

The afternoon dragged on interminably. I was only really conscious of the great pain that seemed to have appeared in the middle of my chest, of recurrent bouts of diarrhoea and the knowledge that somehow I would have to stop Darkie Hurrell from coming to my shattered hideout.

Towards the end of that terrible afternoon I had

another surprise – Miss Bunce reappeared. She came in through the wall door, lugging a large suitcase as I was hanging around in front of the house trying to summon enough courage to make my attempt to head off Darkie. I was still troubled with incipient diarrhoea and gave Bunce as polite a greeting as I could muster before slipping quickly away. I had decided that I would leave by my exit through the hedge near the front gate, walk up the road and wait in the lane where I had encountered Darkie on the previous day. Once again I sat in the tall grass and waited, tormented by a cloud of persistent flies that hovered over me. I broke off a branch and held it over my head, worrying about the torments that the poor cows experienced from these insects.

There was no sign of Darkie Hurrell, only the hump-backed gardener taking a short cut on his way home. The shadows lengthened and the afternoon heat diminished. Still Darkie did not appear. Then I heard, faintly, my mother calling my name. I could tell, even at that distance, that she was cross with me and imagined her leaning slightly forward, her hands on her hips, pink with the exertion of searching for me. Without thinking I took the quickest way back, through Darkie's entrance and into the hideout. I realized my danger only after I stepped into the gloom of the hedge interior. To my surprise, the hurdle house was intact, the rope hung on the tree, the rusty axe was still on the ground. So my uncle had not destroyed my sanctuary, as I had imagined so vividly. But I could not wait and ran down the hollow hedge to emerge behind the mushroom-supported barn.

I located my mother at the back of the house, in the vegetable garden. I knew what would happen. I was scolded, grabbed by one arm and towed into the house for my bath and supper.

It transpired that my mother was cross because, that evening, she had been invited to a whist drive in the village by Mrs Titcombe. Not that she wanted to go, she explained, but Thursa had been so good that it would have been rude to have refused – *and she was going to be late*. I would not be alone in the house, because Miss Bunce would be there and my uncle was not going out until after dark, to look for the poacher.

I certainly did not relish the prospect of being left alone with my uncle, for Miss Bunce was a very inadequate and doubtful ally. My mother, in her haste, seemed not to have considered my feelings on the matter and was certainly too cross to have discussed it with me. I was positively shoved into bed and left, waiting anxiously for the friendly darkness which seemed so slow to come.

As I lay watching the dying sunlight on the whitewashed wall, I turned over in my mind what had happened on this, the worst day of my life. The most surprising thing was that my hurdle house was still intact. It was worrying that Darkie had not turned up, but that might be a good thing. He must have moved on, as he said that he might. He certainly would not have missed our meeting if he had still been around.

Those thoughts were shattered by my uncle's voice calling along the corridor. He was going up to the top of the field to wait ('in case the swine turned in for the night'). Bunce had gone to bed, but he would only be away for an hour or so. If he caught anyone he would come and let me know. He would be going out again after my mother returned.

I heard a door shut and was left in the silence of the old house. The stillness was emphasized by the energetic 'chipping' call of sparrows outside my window.

I realized that if Darkie Hurrell had not gone away,

my uncle would have caught him and beaten him as he did the dogs. I knew, with utter conviction, that he would do this and that his temper would be uncontrollable.

There was nothing that I could do. My helplessness was complete. And then the hate grew within me. It consumed me as it did my uncle. I thought of Father's Wellington boot, of that first beating of the little white dog and how I had wanted to kill my uncle. And I thought of his terrible trap which I *knew* really was lying in the orchard grass between the two white sticks. It was the best place in the whole orchard to set it, because it was only there that you could get through between the unpruned, straggling trees. Later on Uncle Hector would be there as he would not catch Darkie Hurrell at the hideout. I wish that my uncle would get his leg caught in the man-trap, but he would know where it was because of the sticks.

Yet if the sticks were moved he might get caught – and I would like that very much.

That was the one thing I could do. I would have to do it there and then, while my uncle was away at the top of the steep meadow. Without hesitation, I was out of bed, slipped on my blouse and trousers, without my combinations, put on my sandals and crept along the corridor, down the panelled stairs and out through the hall door. It was difficult to open, but in my fury I moved the latch and pushed the heavy carved door ajar and slipped out into a landscape reddened by the setting sun.

I ran along the far side of the elder hedge and into the path between the rows of straggling apple trees. I saw the two sticks, unnaturally white in the fading red light. I was very frightened. I crept up to the sticks. I could only think of the dark jagged teeth concealed in the covering grass. Gingerly I pulled up the nearest stick. Treading carefully, I pushed it into the ground three feet to the left of the other one. The trap was now unmarked. Anyone trying to avoid passing between the sticks would spring the steel jaws.

Then I fled between the trees, so strangely shaped in the sunset light, back along the elder hedge, down the brick path and into the gloomy, empty hall, slamming the door behind me.

I was back in bed in what seemed only a few seconds, breathless, with my heart pumping. At first I felt a profound relief at my safe return and, then, much satisfaction at the thought of my revenge. Later, I heard my uncle return. He called, to say that he was back, had not caught 'the swine' but would do so later on. Again I heard the closing of a distant door.

It was now almost dark and my hatred began to die. But I could no longer stay awake and slipped into sleep with the overwhelming feeling of guilt that, since then, has been the constantly recurring theme of my nightmares.

I can still recall the first manifestation of the nightmare, later that same night, when I stirred in my sleep with a dreadful moaning shriek reverberating in my brain. I was awoken, later, I don't know after how long, by the sound of a closing door – quite near. It was so close that it could only have been from my mother's bedroom. I lay in the darkness worried and frightened in the aftermath of my dream. I knew that it was very late; I could hear a barn owl hunting not far from my window. I began to think of dreadful things, of monks' cowls and my father with his leg trapped. It was much too late for Mother's return from the whist drive. I wished then that my uncle had electric lights in his house. My panic increased when I failed to find the little electric torch that my mother had placed upright beneath my bed in case of emergency. I lay back and tried to think of pleasant things, of my jackdaw and sunlit, flowered meadows, but it was no use. I felt for my torch once more, without success. In total panic I climbed out of bed and after much searching felt, with relief, the smooth glass dome of the torch beneath the dressing table.

By the bright torch beam, I crept out into the corridor and to my mother's bedroom door. The handle turned easily. I called to my mother and shone the torch at the bed. It was empty. The bedclothes were thrown back. I could see the depression that my mother's body had left in the deep feather mattress, felt the lingering warmth of her body and breathed the familiar scent of her toilet water.

It took some moments for me to realize that I was now totally alone. Perhaps my mother had gone to the lavatory (I had come to terms with that problem). But I felt even more frightened in the empty room with the open door and the blackness of the corridor behind. I ran back to my room, slamming the door, and hid beneath the bedclothes to slide into cold, troubled sleep.

11

I awoke to familiar summer sounds and a brilliant sunlit room. I could tell that it was late morning and began slowly to recall my nightmare, Mother's empty bed and, then, the appalling realization of what I had done. Had I really trapped my uncle, as I had set out to do in the grip of my hatred for him?

I slipped on my dressing gown and ran to my mother's room. As I opened the door I saw, to my relief, her shape outlined by the bed covers. She seemed to be awake but did not answer when I spoke. Her face was turned away from me facing the wall. She at last answered me in a small, subdued voice, saying that she was unwell and could not get up. Mrs Titcombe would look after me. Was that why she was up in the night?

'Yes. That was why.'

I had known my mother to be ill before. She occasionally had what she called 'star turns' (which I later learned were migraine). When they came on she would go to bed and send me away, always anxious and frightened.

I returned to my room, washed my face in the porcelain bowl with cold water from the large patterned jug on the dressing table, dressed myself and went downstairs. Mrs Titcombe met me outside the parlour. She was cheerful and told me that she would get my breakfast, as Miss Bunce was still in bed, apparently suffering from nervous exhaustion after her long trip home from Canada.

With my heart in my mouth, I asked her where my uncle was.

'Oh, he's gone out for a long walk on the Downs. Said he needed the exercise.'

So I had not trapped him.

'Did he catch the poacher?' I asked.

'Not that I know of,' Thursa replied. 'But he was up most of the night after him.'

So I was wrong. Uncle Hector had, evidently, not caught Darkie and I had not trapped my uncle. And then I realized what I had to do immediately after breakfast: go into the orchard and move the stick back to its former position.

When I reached the middle of the maze of fruit trees I received yet another shock. The sticks were not there. I walked carefully backwards and looked around for a convenient branch to break off. Then I poked nervously amongst the tall grass for some minutes, but my stick did not encounter the metal of that terrible trap. The grass was trampled and I worried that my uncle would realize that someone had been in that part of the orchard. But I was enormously relieved; perhaps the man-trap had not been there at all. As Darkie had said, my curious uncle was 'having me on' all along.

I walked back, feeling cheerful enough to lark about with the two tethered dogs *en route*. They leapt and barked exuberantly. I would have loved to release them and run with them through the summer fields. They looked so sad when I left that I decided to ask Thursa, who seemed to be in excellent spirits that day, if I could have some scraps of food for them.

It was when I emerged from behind the elder hedge on this errand that I noticed that the pile of Roman stones was gone. I stopped and walked closer: there were the pale squares of white, flattened grass, edged with weeds, where they had stood near the coach house. I could not imagine why they had been moved. Perhaps they had been put in the coach house which, according to my uncle's plan, was to be their final resting place. I pulled open the coach house door, but they were not there. This was very odd. I stood in the half open door pondering what could have happened to them. As I did so, I sensed a dark shape at the edge of my vision; moved my eyes and saw, directly, the jagged teeth and black chain of the man-trap, hanging from its usual place on the wall.

It was like a physical blow to see the horrible device. Why it was again hanging on the wall was beyond my comprehension. I ran back to the dogs and sat close to them on the grass. As they quivered and slobbered over me, I know I thought that, although I could not understand, I would *remember* what had happened. And this was that the trap had not been on the wall when my uncle had said that it was in the orchard and now it was on the wall and not in the orchard. Whatever my mother and Darkie Hurrell had said, I was right: the trap had been in the orchard the previous day. And I had intended that it should catch Uncle Hector during the night.

That was as much as I could cope with. I was still overwhelmed with guilt at my wickedness and I was so worried about my mother. Several times that morning I crept up to her bedroom door and listened. Once I thought I heard faint sobbing, but I couldn't be sure. I just could not understand why she had been taken ill in the night. Perhaps something had happened at the whist drive. But I had imagined them to be sedate affairs, with elderly ladies playing away at rows of green baize tables (as I had once glimpsed through the open door of the church hall). Why had she been out of bed for so long, just to go to the lavatory?

Later in the morning I called through the door and

then opened it to poke my head into my mother's room. There was no movement from the bed, only the instruction given in a flat voice that I should be a good boy and that she would be 'down later'.

It was all very perplexing and I was grateful for the company of Mrs Titcombe (as I had to call her, though I thought of her as Thursa). We lunched together, just the two of us, for Miss Bunce had taken her lunch to her room. Thursa had made a delicious cottage pie, which I adored, and did not go on about 'eating up the vegetables'. I cannot remember what we had for pudding, but distinctly recall the feeling of security which the meal with that buxom countrywoman gave me as we sat in the cream-painted parlour, the only really cheerful room in the entire house.

After our meal Mrs Titcombe observed something to the effect that Bunce's holiday didn't seem to have done her much good and that my uncle had 'gone on a hell of a long walk'. As we sat over the remains of our convivial meal she lit a cigarette (a thing that I had never seen a woman do before). She wondered, further, why her employer seemed to have lost interest in catching the poacher who, in her opinion, didn't do any harm. She implied that she had a good idea who had shot the pigeon.

Thursa evidently had no knowledge of the rat-trap, baited with the single baked bean. It was only at that moment that the full import of that baked bean entered my confused childish mind. Darkie had been around two nights before; I had forgotten that. But I was still comforted by the thought that he had moved on.

Mrs Titcombe's cooking and cheerful company buoyed me up and I left the parlour happier than I had been for two days. The problem was what to do. I was still officially banned from the orchard, had no desire to go up to the top of the steep meadow or to visit the coach house or hang around the other outbuildings. I decided to go to my bedroom. At least I would be near my mother and she was my primary worry that afternoon. I left my door ajar, so that I could hear if she called or came out of the room.

As I slumped idly on my bed, I spotted the yellow corner of a *Rupert* book sticking out of my toy bag. It was a new one; I had not even opened it. The excitements of my visit had quite driven the thought of the book from my mind.

I was soon immersed in the latest goings on in Nutwood. I examined the pictures minutely, envying Rupert his smart check trousers, wondering at the effortless way in which the chums could leap up over the tops of trees and drooling over the delicious little heroine in her frilly dress. I ignored the annoying italicized verses and laboured over the large-lettered prose beneath each square picture. None of the characters, and certainly not Rupert, were the least bit frightened or even particularly worried by their adventures. So different from me and mine. In fact, mine didn't seem like adventures at all. Nothing was clear; I didn't seem to know what was happening half the time. If only Uncle Hector was like the kind old Inventor. *He* was odd too, but always gentle. The only similarities with my life were Rupert's mother and father. He was an only son – I was very pleased about that. Like my parents, Rupert's were comfortable and always interested in their little son. But Mrs Bear never seemed to be ill like my mother and no one ever peed in Mr Bear's Wellingtons.

Still, Darkie Hurrell would have been quite at home in Nutwood. In fact, I had to think very hard to make sure that he wasn't included in some earlier stories, probably standing next to Algy, tall, in queer country clothes, a gun safely tucked under his arm.

I was so absorbed by events at Nutwood that I had not noticed my mother standing at the door. She smiled when I looked up. She was wearing her blue flowered dress, my favourite, and looked pale and tired.

'Shall we go down for tea?' she enquired.

I scrambled eagerly from the bed and ran to the door. My mother caught my shoulder and held me tightly against her while I squirmed in embarrassment, joy and discomfort – her belt buckle was pressing into my nose.

'I have been very silly, James. Please forgive me.'

'Oh, that's all right' – I enjoyed the luxury of magnanimity. But why should Mother apologize for being ill?

Uncle Hector returned while we were taking tea. We heard him open the front door, step into the hall, hesitate outside the parlour. Apprehensively I waited as my mother automatically poured milk into a clean teacup. The door opened as Mother tilted the teapot. I watched the narrow column of amber fluid waver.

A chair was moved and my uncle sat down at my side. I intently examined the pattern of the tablecloth, marshalled cake crumbs with my little finger and became conscious of a corduroyed leg at my side.

'Are you all right?'

As my mother answered my uncle's gruff enquiry, I slid from my chair, without permission, and slipped from the room. The knowledge of my guilt was too great to bear sitting next to Uncle Hector.

I found myself in front of the house, its stone warm in the late afternoon sunshine. It was the time of my meetings with Darkie Hurrell and I thought of the little hurdle house that he had made for me. I would never sit in it again, because Father was coming to fetch us tomorrow, and Uncle Hector would certainly destroy it soon. Then I felt a compelling desire to see it, just once more. The impulse was so strong that I ran all the way, past the mushroom barn and along the tunnel of the hollow hedge.

It was still there: the green canvas neatly tied over the hurdle roof, the sacking walls in place, the rope hung from the tree that I, in fact, had never bothered to climb. I pushed aside the makeshift entrance and crawled inside, to a smell of bruised grass and old sacking, and sat down in the half light, formally, in the exact centre of my sanctuary.

It was not until I turned, in getting up, that I saw what had been lying behind me on the ground. There were two small white skulls, side by side; one of a rabbit (which I already had in my ossuary) and another of a bird. So Darkie had been back. He had kept his promise. I picked up the unexpected additions to my collection and carried them carefully, on the flat of my hand, back down the familiar route to the house and up to my bedroom where I placed them on the chest of drawers next to the *Rupert* book.

I felt a sense of relief. Things weren't so bad after all. Mother was better, if still somewhat strange, and my father was coming to collect us in the morning.

I went to bed early that night, intent on another session with the inhabitants of Nutwood before the evening light faded. I eventually closed the little yellow book and dropped it on the floor by the side of my bed. The sunset light shone on the walls of the familiar little room. As I turned to prepare for sleep I glimpsed the two skulls, reddish in the setting sunlight. I thought of Darkie Hurrell leaving them for me on the previous night and imagined him, tall and silent, moving into my uncle's dark fields and orchard to set his snares and traps. Then a single flash of awful realization shot into my sleepy mind: it was Darkie who had been caught by the waiting metal jaws in the orchard. I slid into another nightmare of terrifying reality in which Uncle Hector savagely beat, with his terrible cudgel, a dark figure lying in tall summer grass.

12

The conviction that I had trapped Darkie Hurrell came to me in a single intuitive flash. At the time I was unable to piece together the confusing happenings of that August night. All I could understand was that the two little skulls meant that Darkie had not left when I thought he had, but that he had, I was convinced, returned to the orchard – to the danger of the man-trap which I had deliberately exposed in the extremity of my hatred for Uncle Hector. Yet I would continue to worry about the events of that night for the rest of my childhood.

These thoughts became a secret compartment of my mind. I would live quite normally, go to school, play with my toys, quarrel, talk with my mother, but always I could slip, unpredictably, into familiar private worries about the night when I had moved the stick in the orchard. I developed a double life – the only way I could survive with my guilt.

This enabled me to cope quite successfully with life. I enjoyed, to the full, the return of my father from his fishing trip and the recommencement of our cosy family life. Despite the doubts engendered by the despised Bonzo postcard, Father had brought me the greatly desired Scottish dirk, which I felt that I had really earned. I cannot now remember how I even knew of the existence of this peculiar weapon. I think that I just liked the way that the words tripped off the tongue and was thrilled to be given the little ebony-handled knife in its engraved metal sheath. Not that I kept it for long. Mother soon confiscated my dirk, in the nicest possible way, by putting it on prominent display at the most inaccessible altitude in our tall, glass-fronted cupboard. My father was rebuked: Mother just could not understand *why* he had bought such a thing for a small boy.

I am ashamed to relate that later that week I climbed up to take down the glorious object, to enjoy the illicit thrill of carrying it in the top of my sock during a juvenile expedition into some nearby fields. How it fell out without my feeling it, I could never understand. I was sent to bed that night without supper, the ultimate punishment, to grieve for the loss of my Scottish bauble and to worry, once again, about a white stick in tall orchard grass, an empty scented bed in a dark room and black steel jaws hanging on a whitewashed wall.

Although I had longed for my father's return I had dreaded the inevitable questions about our stay with Uncle Hector. Fortunately, Father, tanned and full of good humour, was only mildly interested in our visit. He was full of his adventures with Sid Thorpe and had begun to relate them to us, in somewhat confusing detail, during our homeward journey in the familiar blue Austin. But he was concerned that my mother looked so tired and clearly felt twinges of guilt that we had missed our seaside holiday. It was, therefore, with considerable delight that I learned that he had negotiated with my other uncle for a weekend at Sand Bay, including Sandy, but not the jackdaw.

The car journey to the seaside, fifty miles or more, was unbearably long, as I waited with mounting excitement for the first glimpse of the sea. So much was crowded into those two days: splashing in the icy brown water which seemed to take an age to creep across the acres of glistening mud towards the narrow strip of sand which was our beach, digging elaborate channels to try, unsuccessfully, to retain a moat around my sandcastle after the muddly tide had retreated to an infinite distance, eating huge ices, full of gobbets of cream, in the small green-painted hut which served as a café in those innocent days. But even in my happiness I was conscious of the distant figure of my mother, wrapped in a light brown blanket, lying listlessly in a deckchair among clumps of marram grass at the edge of the sand dunes.

She was wearing the intricate silver brooch which my father had brought back as a gift from Scotland. I remember sharing her pleasure as she pinned it on to her white summer dress and, then, a surge of despair when she said that it would replace Darkie Hurrell's brooch which she had left at Uncle Hector's. I had been proud of the ancient ornament which Darkie had given to my mother when he lived in his tarred cottage and had been our constant visitor. For me it was a very special link and I begged that we should go back to Uncle Hector's, much as I hated the prospect, to look for it. No, we would not find it, my mother said with baffling certainty, it was gone, there was no point in searching.

Looking back, I am convinced that our brief holiday was a watershed in my mother's life. It may have been a fault in my early memory, but I cannot recall my mother being ill earlier, except for occasional bouts of migraine. Afterwards, she frequently ailed and from about that time I seem to remember her as middle-aged.

The loss of Darkie Hurrell's brooch perplexed me greatly and revived troubled memories of those last days with Uncle Hector. There were so many strange things that I could not understand: the reappearance of the man-trap, my mother's empty bed, and the screams in my nightmare. Above all, there was the terrible guilt about moving the stick and an unspoken mourning for Darkie Hurrell.

Curiously, it did not occur to me to wonder, in any detailed way, what happened to Darkie. He had been trapped, of that I was convinced, had been caught by my uncle and I would never see him again. My lack of interest seems odd to me now, because I know I was very concerned about the fate of my much loved grandfather. My worries about him embraced not only his metaphysical fate (particularly, whether he had gone to heaven) but also the manner of his passing (whether he had died in what was now my bed and where they had buried him). And I was much younger when my grandfather had died. I can only conclude that there must have been some protective psychological mechanism which prevented me from pursuing such thoughts about Darkie Hurrell. Perhaps my own sense of guilt led to this mental block. As it was, I only worried away about perplexing details when I found myself in the grip of my guilty thoughts.

Despite my initial concern about Grandfather's departure from mortal life, I came to enjoy accompanying my mother on her weekly visits to the family graves. It was part of the cosy round of our family life, as regular and unchanging as cold blancmange and the scullery full of damp clothes on Mondays, and our visit to the library on Fridays, in pursuit of Mother's ceaseless quest for fresh books by Netta Muskett. We visited the churchyard on Wednesday afternoons, in term time, after I had been collected from school by my mother bearing a large bunch of flowers, invariably wrapped in dark blue tissue paper.

I enjoyed feelings of pious solemnity as we scrunched along the gravel path beside the towering church towards the two large family graves, situated side by side on a hillside with a magnificent view of the surrounding countryside. Arrival at the gravesides induced a lightening of my spirits, for as I have said, I had, by this time, come to terms with my grandfather's earthly fate. In fact, I felt a strong sense of family solidarity, at the thought of the subterranean arrays of deceased grandparents, aunts, uncles and cousins, most gratifying to an only child with few close relatives. It was on a damp, early autumn afternoon, when I was watching my kneeling mother carefully trimming the stems of the flowers, that this pleasant feeling suddenly was dispelled by the thought of rows of rotting skeletons beneath the neat clipped grass. I definitely did not want these in my collection.

And then, for the first time, I realized that I did not know what had happened to the body of the lonely man who had helped me build my collection. Had he managed to open the steel jaws and stagger away to die, unnoticed? An image flashed across my mind of a skeleton propped up against the Wayland Smith's Cave. Or had he been secretly buried, at night?

My mother continued the regular snip, snip of her scissors, neatly cutting away at the damp green stems, unaware of the small figure behind her, transfixed with fear. By the time the flowers were arranged in the green pottery vase I had recovered enough to turn away and pretend to look at the carved inscriptions on the other family grave.

We were silent as we walked back to add two bunches of wilting, smelly flowers to the rotting pile near some yew trees in the oldest part of the churchyard. Somehow I sensed that my mother was grateful for our silence and wondered if she too was thinking of Uncle Hector or Darkie Hurrell.

My mother never spoke of Darkie and rarely mentioned

Uncle Hector, although Father occasionally wondered how Darkie was getting on. I think that he missed the yarns in the kitchen about ferrets, long dead country characters, the superstitions to do with magpies, and the regular furred or feathered gifts found hanging on the back door.

Relations with Uncle Hector were very tenuous at this time. The only news that autumn came from Sid Thorpe, who had evidently made up his quarrel with Uncle Hector and now occasionally walked across the fields to my uncle's place.

It appeared from Sid Thorpe's accounts that Uncle Hector was much exercised by the terrible decline of the country, and of the Empire, which were threatened by 'Bolshies'. These were clearly very bad people who were intent on the destruction of King and Country and certainly would not have Jubilee mugs in their glass-fronted cupboards. The 'anti-Bolshies', I can now see, were the followers of Sir Oswald Mosley. I can imagine the enthusiasm with which my Uncle Hector would have embraced Fascism, just as he had enjoyed the General Strike of 1926, in which, I afterwards learned, he had wielded a substantial truncheon to some effect in the East End of London.

It later transpired that Sid Thorpe's visits to our home were, in part at least, engineered by Uncle Hector. It seems that my uncle wished to bury the hatchet with my father, whom he saw as a promising recruit to the anti-Bolshie cause. However, my father was not easily to be reconciled. The incident at St Albans was still an insurmountable obstacle and, furthermore, it turned out that my father did not regard the anti-Bolshies in the same light as Sid Thorpe and my Uncle Hector. To my great confusion he told me that they were very bad people indeed, even worse than the Bolshies themselves. I had no clear idea of what the Bolshies were and eventually decided that they must be the cattle drovers, a very rough lot with red bandana handkerchiefs round their necks, who invaded the town on market days, beating the poor frightened cattle mercilessly with horrid sticks.

His implacable hatred of Bolshies confirmed my belief in Uncle Hector's violence and strengthened my conviction that he had done away with Darkie Hurrell after he had been trapped by my foolish moving of the stick marking the man-trap. This conviction was reinforced later that year when I heard my mother and father discussing something that they had read in the *North Wilts Herald and Advertiser*. Oddly enough my father was amused by the news item which evidently involved Uncle Hector. But Mother was terribly upset by it. I can recall the headline exactly, because my father often referred to it – I suspect to exorcize the memory of his terrible humiliation at St Albans:

THE TEARFUL POACHER

It appeared that Uncle Hector had cornered another of his rustic enemies, on his territory. Somehow or other the village policeman had arrived on the scene to find the intruder, a young farm labourer, blubbering at my uncle's feet. Uncle Hector was severely censured by the magistrates, who had tried the case, for his conduct in so badly beating the young man ('half-killing was the term I remember from the newspaper account as retailed to me by my father).

According to Father the 'silly bugger' was lucky not to have been sent to prison and one day he really would 'do someone in'. But I was convinced that he had already done so and that, in my foolishness, I had been responsible for it.

13

By the time I was seven years old, the last terrible visit to my Uncle Hector's house seemed a very long time ago. Life at Selhurst School for Girls and Boys presented fewer problems, for the vigorous application of Miss Dora's ebony ruler had ensured that I knew my tables and could read with some facility. I was no longer used as an animated punch-bag by the more muscular of the big girls and could defend myself quite successfully against all male contemporaries, except for Raymond Foster. He baffled me, both as a person and as an adversary. This was the cause of my frequent defeats at his hands. He would spend much of his free time licking the top of his wooden pencil box, which I found strangely unnerving. When we fought, I could see in his eyes a desperate desire to win. In a curious way I despised him for this and would just give up.

I had also given up bone collecting by this time; my animal ossuary was now mouldering in a series of damp shoe-boxes in the cellar. But I had learned to work a yo-yo, and was very proud of the achievement. Some recent acquisitions had given my toy collection a strong naval flavour, notably a gun team of rather pop-eyed running sailors, each with a hole in one hand through which a piece of string could be threaded to pull a gun carriage and field gun. I was also amassing a miniature fleet of small metal ships, including *two* battleships, HMS *Hood* and HMS *Warspite*, some three-funnelled cruisers, numerous destroyers and two submarines. I would spend as much as half an hour at a time arranging my fleet in elaborate formations on the parlour carpet and became very cross indeed if my father trod on any of my destroyer patrols.

Despite the passing of time and many juvenile preoccupations, I could still return in my imagination, without warning and at almost any time, to the long Tudor house tucked away in a fold of the Wiltshire Downs. Once again my worries and fears had shifted. In my own way, I believed that I had, slowly and painfully, come to understand what had happened on that terrible August night of the year before. What now frightened me was any possibility of direct confrontation with Uncle Hector, who I feared would know very well who had moved the stick in the long orchard grass while he was waiting to catch Darkie Hurrell at my hurdle house. I tried to allay my fears with the comforting thought that all direct communication had been severed with my fearsome uncle. I now regarded my father's feud with him as a blessing in disguise.

The greatly feared encounter came, one wet summer afternoon, when I was engaged in a complex naval manoeuvre on the parlour floor. This involved me in pushing the numerous tiny grey ships, inch by inch, across the red Turkey carpeting that served as the North Sea, the Straits of Dover and the Dardanelles. At each stage of the manoeuvring I would enjoy the keen pleasure of reviewing my fleet, at sea level so to speak, by lying down at full length with my head on the floor and the dusty carpet smell in my nostrils. I had perfected a technique of squinting through the lashes of my half-closed eyes which gave a most satisfying impression of reality as I gazed at the rows of miniature nautical silhouettes: the long line of protective destroyers, a screen of cruisers and, in the distance, the two mighty battle-ships, their gun turrets pointing in my direction.

It was while I was so engaged that I heard an approaching step and saw the handle turn and the door slowly swing open. Then before me were the unmistakable trouser turnups and muddy boots, more terrifying to me than the whole of the Kaiser's fleet. I turned my head to look upwards into the weather-beaten face of Uncle Hector, looking down at me from an immense height. I felt totally vulnerable. He had only to lift one of those great brown boots to squash my head, like one of the more fragile exhibits in my bird's-egg collection.

I scrambled, sideways, into an uncomfortable sitting position. The blood drained from my face, my hands quivered as I pressed them into the carpet. I could feel the uncomfortably sharp superstructure of HMS *Warspite* pricking me through the blue trouser material. My mouth was too dry even to croak.

'Brought your mother some crab-apples. Got to pick up Bunce. Good luck with the Battle of Jutland.'

And with that, the door closed and he was gone. I waited with bated breath for the distant snick of the closing front door and then slumped face downwards on to the red patterned carpet.

It took me several minutes to recover from the shock of that brief and totally unexpected encounter. I was exhausted. Then slowly I felt a growing sense of well-being. I was still alive. My uncle had not mentioned the stick or the trap. He had even made that remark about the Battle of Jutland. So he did not suspect me.

Such visits by Uncle Hector were rare events and we never visited the Tudor house at Ashbourne. The only news was gleaned from Sid Thorpe, Miss Bunce and occasional items in the *North Wilts Herald and Advertiser*.

It appeared that Uncle Hector's flirtation with Fascism was largely theoretical in nature, really only an excuse for more frequent, violent fantasies in which he thrashed various public figures in a loose-box. On at least one occasion, however, Sid Thorpe and my uncle had ventured on to the streets in support of Sir Oswald Mosley. Not in our little market town, of course (there must have been little scope for Fascism in North Wiltshire even in those days), but in the capital itself.

The episode was related to my father by Sid Thorpe, whose renewed loyalty to Uncle Hector was becoming distinctly frayed. I learned of the events first by my usual strategy of lurking outside the door and later from frequent gleeful repetitions by my father.

On the day in question the pair of them drove to Swindon Junction and there boarded the early train to arrive in London in good time for the Mosleyite march. Unfortunately, they ran into stiff opposition (I imagined from cattle-driving Bolshies) somewhere in the East End. Uncle Hector and Sid Thorpe became separated from the main body of marchers and found themselves hemmed into a side street behind a line of policemen. There they were subjected to some very colourful and imaginative abuse, delivered at short range by several formidable Cockney harridans. Because of his distinctive, and distinguished, appearance Uncle Hector received the full force of it.

Shocked and thrilled by the enormity of it all, I learned that my uncle had been likened to a 'lump of shit on broomsticks' and his facial appearance compared with that of 'a cow's backside, with two currants for eyes'. Even more shocking, my father frequently repeated these two phrases, hence my accurate memory of them. This seemed to me at the time to be the supreme example of adult hypocrisy. I was still troubled with the more repellent aspects of animal and human excretion and reproduction. I took a scholarly interest all the same in the vocabulary of the cattle-drovers during their regular, weekly invasion of our town, and had memorized quite a comprehensive list of blasphemies and obscenities. Yet when I tested one, in a purely experimental way, in the presence of some of my mother's matronly friends I was severely slapped on the legs and sent to my room. It was all very perplexing, especially as my father often used the word 'bugger', usually in connection with Uncle Hector.

My uncle had apparently made light of his humiliation by saying that his tormentors 'were not out of the top drawer' (to me, a most mysterious phrase, which had prompted my father to wonder which damned drawer my uncle thought that he came from). Yet I could imagine, and still relish the extent of Uncle Hector's verbal torment by the good women of the East End. He must have been apoplectic. An infinity of revenge in the loose-box would not have been enough to extinguish that humiliation.

Although shocked by the hypocrisy of my father's repetition of the unbelievably rude phrases used against my uncle, I still found them strangely comforting. I suppose that they helped to exorcize the memory of that terrifying figure; the cause of the dark fears that still troubled me and of my own guilty act. These worries were like a cancer in my mind, but a benign one which I had walled off, so that I could cope with all the other problems which beset my life.

My difficulties were compounded when, at the age of eight, I was transplanted from the relative sanctuary of Selhurst School for Girls and Boys to the elementary school. There were only two of us who continued our education by that route, for the other boys went to various preparatory schools. This, it was explained to me, was because my father's business was not prospering and money could not be found to pay for me to go to a preparatory school. The only comfort was that Raymond Foster would not be accompanying me in the next stage of my education. What I did not know, but soon discovered, was that there were far worse things in the world than that pencil-box-licking fiend. There was 'Fatty' Higgins who used to ambush me on the way home from school and bully me unmercifully. There were the long echoing corridors, the unspeakable stinking lavatories, the rows of uncomfortable desks in ugly Victorian classrooms, the smelly cloakrooms that, on rainy days, were piled with damp, steaming clothes from which, with great difficulty, I had to extract my own blue gaberdine raincoat and school cap. Some of the boys had shaven heads covered with purple spots and, once, my mother found a flea on my vest. Selhurst School for Girls and Boys was now a distant vision of heaven. Miss Dora seemed like a kindly angel, her ebony ruler a golden wand.

After a few days, I had had enough and rebelled. One rainy September morning I clung to the front door frame refusing to budge. I was eventually towed, weeping, all the way to that redbrick hell by my poor upset mother, only to be exposed to even worse jeering and bullying by my appalling fellow pupils.

My private nightmare had now been overtaken by what, at the time, seemed like even more hideous reality.

I betrayed my secret, for the first time, to Fatty Higgins. He had waylaid me not far from the school gates. Fatty was two years older than me, as many stone heavier and there was little I could do to resist his regular assaults. He was always raggedly dressed, his head a mosaic of purple-stained impetigo spots. I think his sadism was part of a broader scheme of class warfare against the children of the *petite bourgeoisie*.

Fatty's torturing usually involved throwing me, face downwards, on the ground and then kneeling on my back so that I suffered a continual splitting pain. He had many further refinements on this basic theme. He could scrouge my face in gravel, or push it downward on to asphalt to flatten my nose, he could twist the skin on my arm in opposite directions (to produce the intense pain we called Chinese fire), he could half strangle me or pull my ears until I feared they would part company with my head. He usually had one or two comrades with him to offer advice and encouragement or to assist him if in my desperate struggles to escape I showed the slightest chance of succeeding.

It was in the early stages of one of Fatty's torturing sessions that I attempted to stave him off by promising that I would tell him a great secret if he would only stop.

'What sort of secret?'

'It's about how I really killed someone,' I croaked.

'You? How?'

'With a man-trap,' I gabbled as the pain subsided. 'My uncle set a man-trap and I moved the stick that marked it in the grass.'

'Who did you catch?'

'A poacher. An old poacher.'

'What did you do with him?'

'My uncle beat him.' I hesitated. ' . . . I think he did!'

My hesitation was enough fully to confirm Fatty's disbelief.

'Liar,' he hissed.

The pain was worse that time than it had ever been and I still remember reeling off, sobbing, to the jeers of

112

Fatty and his friends. I knew that somehow I had betrayed Darkie Hurrell and wished that he had been alive to protect me. If I really was a liar he could still do so.

Strangely, I found it difficult to remember what Darkie had looked like. In my memory he was becoming indistinguishable from a character in a Rupert story, dressed in a curiously long jacket with a gun under one arm.

I never told my parents about the bullying. For one thing, it would go against the rigid schoolboy code which, improbably, I must have imbibed at Selhurst School for Girls and Boys and, for another, I strongly suspected that any attempts to obtain justice would only result in much worse treatment later.

Eventually my tormentor lost interest in me and took to bullying another victim, a new boy, Dennis Bowen, the local jeweller's son. There was nothing I could do to protect Bowen, but I used to hang around at a safe distance, and worry, as I had about the dog beatings at Ashbourne. When the coast was clear I would walk home with the snivelling wretch, to try and cheer him up. However, my kindness was not wholly disinterested, for I was in love with his mother. The fact was that to me Mrs Bowen was the closest approximation to Ginger Rogers in our small country town. I had developed a deep passion for Miss Rogers, since I had seen two of her films (with Fred Astaire) on occasional Saturday afternoon visits to the cinema with my mother. Mother was amused when I had rhapsodized on Mrs Bowen's matchless beauty; she snorted something about the jeweller's wife being 'brassy' and, later, treacherously retailed my confession to some of her amused, ugly cronies. But I didn't care; I thought Mrs Bowen exceptionally beautiful and was quite prepared to exploit her son's misfortunes to catch a glimpse of his mother's golden wavy hair, heavily powdered cheeks and crimson lips, and to sniff at the exciting perfume which she exuded so freely.

My friendship with Bowen blossomed and soon I was calling him Dennis. He was a neat, shy boy, with fair hair like his mother (which showed that hers was not bleached, as my mother claimed). He had a very large railway set, which his father had set up on planks around two sides of their attic.

The Bowens also had something which was very special – what they called 'the launch': a wooden river cruiser moored some miles away on a quiet reach of the Upper Thames. On the bank they had a small, green hut, 'the chalet', set in a neat square of closely-mown grass delimited by a row of neat white sticks, and a length of sagging white rope. Once they took me down with them for a weekend, after the shop had closed on a Saturday evening. It was then that I saw the object of my adoration in a one-piece bathing costume, and rubber hat. I nearly swooned at the sight of those glorious white limbs (there was no nonsense about female suntanning in those days).

Dennis Bowen was a very truthful boy. Unlike me, he would never lie to get out of trouble at school and would instantly own up when justly accused. I think it was for this reason that I felt compelled to tell him the story of the man-trap and my involvement in the affair at Ahsbourne, for I had been surprised, and very disappointed, by Fatty Higgins's disbelief.

As I started to tell Dennis about Uncle Hector and the man-trap, I noticed him look away. We were peering into the water at the time to watch the minnows swim into our trap (an empty wine bottle with the bottom knocked out, baited with a piece of cheese), but he had been watching my face as I started my story. Then Bowen began to shake his head.

'I don't believe you.'

'You're making it up,' he muttered angrily, clearly outraged that I should deliberately lie to him about something as improbable as involvement in a murder.

Bowen never regarded me in the same light again. I was naturally a little upset about his changed attitude, but, strangely, experienced a deep feeling of release at his scepticism. In some way it dissolved my sense of guilt and made the terrible events at Ashbourne seem improbable. Yet I knew that I had somehow cheapened the memory of the strange dark friend of my earlier childhood.

14

Just before Christmas of that year – I think it must have been 1937 – I suffered a grievous loss: the jackdaw, who had been my constant companion, died. He was not in his green-painted wooden cage when I returned from school on the last day of term, nor did he appear, as he invariably did, when I called his name on that cold winter's evening. I found his body the following morning, coated with hoar frost, beside a hedge next to our vegetable garden. He had been shot in the back of his neck, by an air rifle according to my father.

I was devastated by the killing, but as the holidays had begun I was able to give full vent to my grief with frequent bouts of weeping and snivelling, without any worries about being seen crying at school. Strangely, for she had borne the death of Sandy with equanimity, my mother was almost as upset as I was and, for the first time since we had last stayed at Ashbourne, mentioned Darkie Hurrell. I had almost forgotten that it was he who had brought the tiny chick for me to tend so many years before. Abandoning recently acquired inhibitions about hugging my parents I clung to my mother in total misery. It was then that she spoke of Darkie. I remember that she said what a good friend he had been to me and I am sure that she mentioned the Roman brooch that Darkie had given her. What I cannot be sure about, because at the time it didn't make sense, was that she said that she had 'left the brooch with Darkie'. Looking back, I don't think I imagined this because I recall the image that flashed into my troubled mind of my mother handing the brooch to the old poacher as he stood near a tall hedge with his shotgun under his arm. My mother's whispered remark made no sense. Certainly it did not convey to me at the time the obvious implication: that she must have seen Darkie Hurrell *after I had* on the terrible day when I believed that he had been trapped and killed.

I chipped away a grave for Jack in the hard frosty soil and buried him in a shoe-box coffin lined with cotton wool. On the following day, Sunday, I asked if we could go to church (a rare event, for my father had a strong antipathy to religion) and prayed for the soul of my old bedraggled jackdaw.

Christmas that year was made dismal by the loss of my pet. My presents were also less than satisfactory. I found it difficult to get the hang of the Meccano set and when I managed to assemble a bridge, crane or aeroplane it never seemed to have a convincing appearance of reality. The conjuring set was also a disappointment; I could not manipulate half the tricks and the others seemed to disintegrate in my hands. The King's Speech was infinitely long and Boxing Day was an anticlimax.

I dreaded the return to school, plodding with soaking shoes through the slushy streets, being shoved about in the damp crowded cloakrooms and shouted at by uncongenial teachers with uncouth northern voices who attempted to suppress our Wiltshire burring.

I particularly detested the headmaster, a small sandy-haired man with a grating voice who walked as though he had been shot in the stomach a decade earlier. He was dedicated to the destruction of our native dialect and phraseology. One of his more distressing practices was to select a word and to make the entire school, class or handful of surprised pupils trapped in cloakroom or

117

playground chant repeatedly his version of the pronunciation of the selected word. This would continue for days, or even weeks, until every child could repeat the word to his satisfaction.

He ran a protracted crusade concerning the pronunciation of the second month of the year.

'FebRUary, not FebURary,' he would shout in a voice which must have been moulded somewhere on the Lancashire/Yorkshire border.

'FebRUUaary,' we would bawl back with the full force of our lungs, trying unsuccessfully to mimic the clipped northern tones.

It was all very puzzling, for I was sure that my mother would certainly consider the headmaster to be 'common'. However, she knew very little of what went on at that awful school and never, as far as I can remember, went near the place.

Yet despite the headmaster's efforts I had, in order to survive, to adopt the speech and attitudes of my contemporaries at school. This distressed my mother as much as it annoyed the headmaster. As a consequence, I was sent, on Saturday mornings, to elocution classes given by a genteel, dark-haired young woman who lived in a rented bed-sitting room on the ground floor of a large Victorian house, some half a mile from my home.

My reluctant companions were Dennis Bowen and another fellow pupil, Skinny Ellis, notable in our eyes for his large collection of Dinky Toy cars. We were all deeply ashamed by this exercise in provincial snobbery and dreaded what would happen if Fatty Higgins should ever get to know that we were forced to recite such epics as:

Godfrey Gordon Gustavus Gore
Never could learn to shut the door...

On the way home we used to counteract these humiliating and embarrassing, totally soppy proceedings by much exaggerated punching and shoving, shouting in the broadest patois, scrumping apples, stoning cats and playing marbles in the gutter.

The net effect of all this was that I developed four different modes of speech. The first was that of the playground, the genuine Wiltshire article (in which, for example, the request to kick a ball in one's direction to score a goal would be: 'Yer. Oxun oover yer and U'll slammocks un droo thie sticks'). The second was the classroom version. This was less extravagant than the first and showed some bleak northern influences from the headmaster's ever-increasing list of chanted words. Then there was the language that I used at home, largely to avoid the dreadful stigma of 'commonness' so greatly feared by my mother. This, I now realize, was very far from standard English and to metropolitan sophisticates would scarcely have been distinguishable from the speech of yokels. The fourth category was that of the elocution class and bore no relation to reality, except when expressed in the beautifully modulated voice of the vicar's wife. I suppose the closest approximation to an exponent in our family was Uncle Hector, although his gruffness made it difficult to discern.

Despite the unmitigated horrors of school, I nevertheless adapted – like Little Lord Fauntleroy in a band of cut-throats. My home was now a blissful haven. On return from school there would be a glass of warm milk, a plate of Osborne biscuits and the prospect of *Children's Hour* on the wireless. On Thursdays, unopened copies of the *Dandy* and the *Beano* would be lying on the hall table, crisp with their unique printer's smell and the promise of fresh exploits from Desperate Dan, Keyhole Kate and

Korky the Kat. Then there was the possibility of another re-creation of George VI's Coronation, with the glorious golden-painted coach and rather inadequate detachments of brilliantly painted Guardsmen and Horse Guards, or yet another naval exercise on the parlour floor.

On autumn days or summer evenings I would mooch about the nearby fields collecting horse chestnuts, catching minnows, damming streams, searching for newts and grass snakes, thrilled by the flashing brilliance of a kingfisher or the glimpse of a hunting sparrowhawk. The necessity of keeping alert for gamekeepers and rough boys, especially Fatty Higgins and his gang, gave a spice of danger and the excitement of stalking them from a safe distance. I could not remember the time when I had not known the names of most of the wild birds and where to take their eggs. This was Darkie's legacy to me, unrecognized as his memory faded and the daytime fears of my guilty involvement with the man-trap subsided beneath my realization of the improbability of it all. Only at night did confused nightmare versions return in which I was terrified by small animal skulls bathed in reddish light and oppressed with a terrible weight of guilt. Even these were becoming infrequent, recurring only as fever dreams or during rare bouts of midnight wakefulness.

Uncle Hector intruded only occasionally into my life, with his characteristic, abrupt visits bearing inadequate gifts from the countryside – and once a framed copy of Kipling's *If*. The poem was inexpertly mounted in a battered frame and made very little sense. It greatly annoyed my father, who apparently had been planning a similar present, but had deferred giving it to me until a later birthday.

I gathered from my mother that Uncle Hector thoroughly approved of my attendance at the terrible elementary school. Mother considered this to be a typical example of his perversity, but I did not agree, for I had not forgotten the dog beatings and knew that this was exactly the fate he would have arranged for me. However, I still remembered vividly and with pleasure our visit to Avebury and his talk about the people who had built the great stone circle and the strange conical hill nearby. I would often beg to be taken there on weekend outings in the car and vastly enjoyed scrambling up Silbury Hill, ahead of my puffing father, to sit alone for a few moments with the sound of skylarks all around in the clear downland air.

It was while we were on one of our weekend drives that Father made a casual remark which exploded in my mind. It was a late summer day and so hot that we had wound down all the car windows to get the benefit of the very modest draught of air created by my father's maddeningly slow driving. I remember his words exactly.

'Oh. By the way, I met Sid Thorpe yesterday.'

He paused, carefully changed gear and continued.

'Says he saw Darkie Hurrell at the cattle market, last week . . . or at least he thought he did.'

I was agog with excited interest.

'What did he say? Where has he been for so long?'

'Well, that's the funny thing. Sid couldn't catch up with him.'

'Why not?'

'Sid said that he saw him on the other side of the sheep pens, but there were so many people at the auction that he couldn't get round.'

'Well?'

'When he looked again he was gone.'

Father pondered the matter and continued.

'It's funny he's not been to see us if he has come back.'

For weeks I waited expectantly for Darkie to appear in the kitchen or to find a rabbit hanging on the back door knob. I hung around the cattle market, despite my intense dislike of the place, and was always on the look-out for the tall dark figure whether walking through the town streets or roaming the familiar surrounding fields and woods. But there was no sign of Darkie Hurrell.

The troubled years at school dragged on. The bullying subsided only to be replaced by a fresh torment in the form of enforced combat, usually against equally reluctant adversaries. These awful encounters, the result of trivial playground disputes, would be heralded by great shouts of 'Fight Fight' that would be taken up by all the children in earshot. Then I would find myself pressed forward at one side of a ring of pushing excited children urging instant assault on a red-faced, often ragged child at the other side of the heaving circle. The outcome was usually inconclusive as we sprang at each other punching, kicking and scratching, but I often returned home bruised with torn clothes to be lectured by my mother about becoming a hooligan and, later, by my father on the manly techniques of 'standing up for myself', which, according to him, were all encompassed in the ridiculous framed poem that Uncle Hector had given me.

I realized at that time that my father was worried about the business and shared with him the misery he felt on the occasions when he had to sack another man who had joined the firm in my grandfather's time. I also knew that something was very wrong with the world beyond our quiet Wiltshire town. There was talk of war and my parents would listen subdued and worried, to solemn voices on the wireless. Father veered between despair and rage, sometimes shouting about there being 'only one good Hun . . . a dead one'. My military and naval engagements on the parlour floor achieved urgent relevance and I was delighted to be able to add to the forces at my disposal the very latest and terrible machines of war – three Dinky Toy Gloster Gladiator fighter planes.

I was ten years old when I heard a flat, tired voice, on the wireless set that had brought so much childhood pleasure, announcing that the country was at war with Germany. Without hesitation I ran along two empty streets to stand outside the green corrugated iron gates of the drill hall, in the expectation of seeing squadrons of tanks and columns of marching men emerge *en route* for the Front to fight the ancient enemy. But the gates remained firmly shut and eventually I slunk home, kicking the leaves in the gutter, to a familiar family supper.

I had no doubts about the outcome of the war. I had assumed charge of the *Daily Express Map of the Western Front* which was now a prominent feature of the sitting room wall, and derived considerable pleasure from sticking the miniature paper flags on to pins and then placing them in opposing rows along the Maginot and Siegfried Lines. Then after months of boring inactivity, while I waited impatiently to move the French and British flags forward, I had to shift the German flags sharply to the left on the map and then forward and those of the Allies back and back until I gave up in despair.

In the year of Dunkirk I left the elementary school and, against all expectations, gained a place in the grammar school. Despite rationing, clothing coupons and my father's business problems, Mother managed to buy me a school uniform. We celebrated this by a visit, on the train, to Oxford. There, in my new cap and blazer, I saw for the first time strange figures hurrying along damp pavements in mortar boards and fluttering black gowns.

An old gentleman in a tea shop gave me a shilling when I said that I wanted to wear one of those gowns. When he asked me what I would study I answered immediately 'History' (the only subject I was good at at school), which yielded another shilling and strengthened my resolve still further, for I could not imagine that they would study birds, or encourage bird's-nesting, at Oxford University.

It was at this time that Uncle Hector came into his own as leader of the Ashbourne Local Defence Volunteers. The Tudor house was the nerve centre of operations. Shotguns, .22 rifles and even airguns were collected and stacked in one of the flint outbuildings. Uncle Hector greatly enjoyed bossing about a motley collection of increasingly truculent farm labourers and village trades-men. More than anything else he was thrilled by the opportunity to devise a bizarre succession of unorthodox lethal devices which eventually culminated in an elaborate invention that incorporated a large quantity of dynamite. The explosives were commandeered at gunpoint from a nearby quarry, by my uncle and a carefully selected detachment of three mentally unbalanced villagers. The outraged owner was forced to abandon his quarrying activities for weeks until he replaced his store of explosive.

My uncle's secret weapon, for which he required the dynamite, was a sort of extended booby trap. The idea was that once the Germans' line of advance had been determined, the device would be quickly strung out for several hundred yards in front of the enemy, carefully concealed among thistles, clumps of stinging nettles and couch grass in neglected pastureland on the western boundary of the parish. The first infantryman or para-trooper to blunder into a trip wire would detonate the entire stock of the unfortunate quarry owner's dynamite.

The devastating effect of the multiple explosions would, according to my uncle's plan, be quickly followed up by a fusillade of shotgun blasts, petrol bombs and home-made mortar bombs fired from drain pipes.

My uncle had decided to string out his lethal booby trap regularly so that his suicide squad would become accustomed to handling such a quantity of explosives and, in addition, would become ever more proficient at deploying it under fire. But he forgot to inform the owner of the pastures, Charlie Horton, of the terrible danger that lay hidden in his neglected lower meadows. Charlie was of an indolent disposition and at four o'clock each afternoon would call in his herd of Friesian cows from the farmyard gate. At this signal the beasts would obligingly plod towards the muddy yard, and patiently await admission to the milking parlour. On the day in question, Charlie Horton called in his herd while Uncle Hector's suicide squad were practising a quick 'recce' to establish the exact position of a hypothetical group of advancing German paratroopers.

Charlie was reputedly leaning on his farmyard wall, drinking a cup of tea, when the leading cows exploded. The explosions continued intermittently for some minutes, exactly as Uncle Hector had intended. His secret weapon might, in fact, have had considerable military potential; it was only the unfortunate timing of its use that caused the subsequent furore.

My father was fully informed of the débâcle at Ashbourne by Sid Thorpe, who had been marginally involved in the affair, and by a cryptic news item which appeared in the *North Wilts Herald and Advertiser*, at that time sadly reduced to a two-page shadow of its former bulk by the wartime paper shortage.

Father greatly enjoyed my uncle's predicament. It

turned out that Uncle Hector had no military authorization for recruiting his rustic partisans, no powers to commandeer dynamite and certainly no authority to leave considerable quantities of explosive lying about in his neighbour's fields. However, by far the greatest humiliation was the response of the army officer who was sent to investigate Uncle Hector and his subordinates. This 'regular' was outraged when he discovered that a former trooper in the yeomanry ('a damned ranker') should have the temerity to assume the command of men, even Wiltshire yokels.

From that time forward Father invariably referred to the violator of his Wellington boot as 'the damned ranker'. This pettiness annoyed my mother, but Father had another score to settle for he knew, only too well, who Uncle Hector was getting at when he sneered about the 'temporary gentlemen' who had gained commissioned rank in the First World War.

Unlike my father, I was appalled and frightened when I heard of the dreadful goings on in Charlie Horton's lower fields. Even at the advanced age of eleven I was still greatly affected by any kind of animal suffering (I once shed a few tears in the Astoria Cinema during a Saturday morning showing of *Lassie Come Home* and was ribbed about it for weeks by Skinny Ellis). The thought of the blasted black and white corpses of Charlie Horton's cows haunted me. I also remembered the jagged teeth of the man-trap hanging by its black chain on the whitewashed wall, what seemed like so very many years before, and wondered whether Sid Thorpe really had seen Darkie Hurrell near the sheep pens that market day.

Uncle Hector retired like a sulking Achilles after the Ashbourne cattle massacre. He was considerably out of pocket. My father reckoned that it would have cost him at least thirty-five pounds a cow to repay Charlie Horton for the slaughter of ten of his Friesians.

It was not for many weeks that I saw Uncle Hector again. He was taking tea with my mother when I came in from school. I rarely looked at him directly, but I took in at a single glance how much he had aged. To me he had always been in middle years, but now he seemed old. I suppose that he was – he could not have been far off seventy – but he had been so erect and energetic. His hair still retained a colour of faded gold. It was his hands that revealed the truth. They were still strong and there was no sign of tremor, but I sensed ageing bones beneath a mottled skin and saw protruding veins like roots of an ancient beech in shallow downland soil.

It was at the time of the siege of Tobruk. I was much excited by the latest news from the Western Desert, especially the breakout of the British garrison and the retreat of the Afrika Korps. I was looking forward to the rare experience of advancing the paper Union Jacks on the yellow sands of the *Daily Telegraph War Map of the Middle East* which had replaced the one that had recorded the humiliation of Dunkirk. Uncle Hector, however, did not share my enthusiasm and barked out something about Rommel being a 'splendid chap' before launching forth on the merits of the 'plucky' Boer farmers who had been the adversaries in his war. It was treason. Yet I understood how the humiliation of the Ashbourne massacre must have eroded my uncle's idiosyncratic patriotism.

Uncle Hector's visits were infrequent during those war years, for his 'bull-nose' was laid up for want of petrol, and he hated sitting on the uncomfortable slatted seats with fellow villagers in the *Queen of the Hills*. But there was one visit which I recall vividly. My mother was out

127

when he called. I was confronted in the parlour, huddled in front of an inadequate fire, struggling unsuccessfully with the hideous obscurities of algebra. I felt the familiar surge of fear at the sound and then the sight of the tall figure standing at the open door. This increased when Uncle Hector stepped towards me.

'I've wanted to get you on your own,' he growled. 'Always tied to your mother's apron strings.'

I backed away. This was awful. I knew what he would say. The memory of the trap flooded back. He took another step towards me.

'Self abuse,' he grated in a husky whisper. 'Terrible thing at your age.'

I backed away in considerable confusion, as he recited a list of very unpleasant symptoms ranging from permanent fatigue to premature ageing, the price of unchecked sensual pleasure.

The pattern of the Turkey carpet dominated my mind as I gazed downwards, neck and ears reddening. Then with a grunt my uncle turned and strode from the room.

Despite my confusion, I knew exactly what I wanted to do. I ran upstairs to the bathroom, carefully locked the door and stood before the wash-basin, looking in the mirror. Then, still flushed and excited at the prospect of self abuse, I pulled the ugliest grimace I could manage and cursed myself with the worst obscenities which I could muster.

It was mildly diverting, but hardly pleasurable and certainly not thrilling. I could not conceive how it could produce premature ageing. It was another year before I knew what my uncle had feared.

But there were lesser depravities: smoking De Ritz cigarettes with Bowen in the garden shed, apple nogging, brooding on the distant memory of Tessy's revelation, primitive dirty jokes.

Despite these distractions, I prospered at school. I was never far from the top of the class, regularly won the J.J. Stebbings History Prize and was the boy wonder of the town's Natural History Club.

The Wiltshire countryside became an armed camp. Flint roads and chalky downland tracks were churned by the wheels and tracks of countless engines of war. Voices from Cincinnati and Denver mingled with the accents of Cockney and Geordie in town and village streets that had not known the clash of arms since Saxon times. Thousands of acres of downland went under the plough. The great flocks of sheep and their lonely guardians disappeared with the destruction of the sweet downland turf. Amidst all this I ploughed on with surds and the pluperfect, 'Distress and Discontent After 1815', kinetic theory and *Henry V*. Then the countryside was quiet again and once more we moved our paper flags across the map of Europe.

The VE Night celebrations were an anticlimax. It was not only the modest nature of the festivities in our quiet corner of Wiltshire, but the consciousness of my callow innocence amidst the robust vulgarity of the singing women and soldiers in the market square. At sixteen I was ashamed of my dark-haired, sallow appearance and longed to be fair and pink-skinned as I lurked in shadows at the edge of the excited singing mob.

15

The dreary aftermath of war marked the end of my childhood and the growth of adolescent discontents. Home, which had seemed so spacious and comfortable, shrank to shabby inadequacy; our town, formerly so busy and important, was now scruffy and provincial. It was not just the drab austerity of the times. There was the realization of the inevitable ordinariness, the crushing dullness, the asphyxiating stodginess of life in a small Wiltshire town.

It was all epitomized by my parents' musical tastes: Henry Hall and his Orchestra, heard on our fretworked, ten-year-old wireless set, the Palm Court Orchestra playing selections from Gilbert and Sullivan on wet Sunday evenings. I wanted to blow the whole damned lot to hell. And, in a way, I would – but not then. All I could do was survive in the familiar environment of childhood like a slug in a wilting bunch of flowers.

From sheer boredom, I took to lying. For weeks at a time I would deliberately manufacture untruths and then maintain their veracity against all probability in increasingly complex arguments with my mother. I indulged in malicious gossip and occasionally took to petty pilfering from the small stores of money that my mother maintained in scattered caches, in cupboards and drawers, to pay the milkman, the newspaper boy, the coalman, the baker and the insurance agent. This caused some satisfying minor furores and often led to poor Florrie being regarded with unjust suspicion.

I acquired an improbable ally in adolescent rebellion and boredom – my pencil-box-licking enemy from the days of Selhurst School, Raymond Foster. He had gone to prep school and then to Radley. There, in the first term of the sixth form, he had been involved in a mildly sensational affair involving two Land Girls in an old bicycle shed in a quiet corner of the school grounds. Raymond's expulsion from Radley had been handled most tactfully by his family and, at the time, we were all unaware of the reasons for his abrupt appearance in our little grammar school. It was not until I was in my last undergraduate year at university that I learned from a former Radley man of the reasons for Raymond's departure from the school.

The Fosters lived in a beautiful Georgian house set on a hillside, in large grounds, on the outskirts of the town. His father was a prosperous solicitor who had acquired a number of additional business interests, including a large tannery, a mill and a farm or two. There was no doubt that the Fosters were a cut above my family. My poor mother, who had been very confused by the abrupt change in attitudes of her adolescent son, was very pleased at my renewed acquaintance with Raymond Foster and did all she could to promote our friendship.

Raymond Foster was a very precocious seventeen-year-old (he was, in fact, a year older than I was, but had somehow slipped a year so that we were contemporaries at school). There was not only his carnal knowledge of girls and his consumption of alcohol, but also his mysterious familiarity with contemporary artistic trends. I had no idea how he acquired such sophisticated insight. My aesthetic horizons at that time were bounded by our George Morland prints in their wholesome Hogarth frames, by my father's literary tastes (notably his enthusiasm for *John Halifax, Gentleman*) and Mother's preference for selections from *The Desert Song* or *The Student Prince*, preferably rendered by Albert Sandler and the Palm Court Orchestra. Raymond Foster, on the other hand, knew about such exciting mysteries as Pointillism, Vorticism, Cubism and Futurism. He knew the difference between Subjective Realism and Subjective Idealism, the significance of *Die Neue Sachlichkeit*, even Emil Nolde, 'Nordic Sensibility' and Cocteau. I later discovered Raymond's secret weapon – a battered copy of Herbert Read's *Art Now*, which he had been lent by the art master at Radley and had failed to return. However, at the time I was greatly impressed by his grasp of contemporary artistic trends. I had only just heard of Surrealism (*Surréalisme* as he pronounced it) and had no idea what it meant. But the important thing was, there was *absolutely nothing* of this kind abroad in North Wiltshire at that time and such artistic pretensions became an essential weapon in our two-pronged attack on the native *petite bourgeoisie*.

At first, I faced considerable difficulties in my attempts to keep up with Raymond's savoir faire, so effectively cultivated from his illicit copy of *Art Now*. However, I soon developed my own strategy by repeated visits to the exhibitions organized in the town hall by the Council for the Encouragement of Music and Arts, and by the considerable expenditure (2s 6d a copy) involved in building up an impressive knowledge of Edward Burra, Henry Moore, Victor Pasmore and Graham Sutherland from the row of buff and white copies of the *Penguin Modern Painters* that were the pride of my small bookcase.

The second prong of our cultural onslaught on the

unsuspecting North Wiltshire of 1946 resulted from my initiative. It had seemed to me that our prime target should be on the musical front, for I was now suffering acutely from the outpourings of Messrs Hall and Sandler and their orchestras relayed through our ageing wireless set and, even more, a surfeit of selections from the *Maid of the Mountains* played on our wind-up, HMV table-top gramophone. Fortunately, I discovered that my parents had a strong antipathy to dance bands, especially those of Joe Loss and Nat Gonella. This was a promising lead, and I made a couple of 2s 11d purchases of their records from the local music shop. It was while I was contemplating a third addition to my collection that I came across a black-labelled Brunswick disc of one Art Hodes and his band playing 'Indiana'. I had discovered jazz, the perfect antidote to my musical torments. Together, Raymond Foster and I busily acquired a growing pile of Parlophone, HMV and Brunswick records which yielded the lusty vigour of Muggsy Spanier, Louis Armstrong, Duke Ellington and Bessie Smith. Our poor parents were shattered – exactly what we had in mind.

By the time I was seventeen we had acquired a few youthful, spotty disciples and, to the disgust of the proprietor, spent much time in drinking cups of lukewarm *Camp* coffee, lolling on the wicker-work chairs in the pale green setting of the Astoria Café. Our hair was now excessively long, at least by the standards of the time, and I wore a dark green shirt and red tie (both of which I had dyed myself) and a fawn duffel coat which I had bought for thirty-five shillings. Occasionally we would meet in Raymond's bedroom in order to satirize our more conventional fellow-pupils, to read the poems of Auden, Spender and MacNeice and to discuss such artistic innovations as reached our quiet corner of Wiltshire. It was at this time I discovered I had an unsuspected facility with the pseudo-intellectual phrase. I was particularly proud of 'a certain primitive awareness', which I applied to a reproduction of a baffling abstract in the latest copy of *Studio*.

It was all quite enjoyable, but there were snags. One drawback was a certain lack of progress with girls. We seemed positively to repel them. In fact, I suspect that Raymond Foster deliberately changed into what he called his 'young farmer's outfit' (hacking jacket and cavalry twill trousers) to achieve his successes in that direction.

I also felt considerable personal diffidence in my relations with Raymond Foster. He was fair and pink-skinned and emphasized my dark, gipsy looks; he always seemed to win, even in the school games he affected to despise; worst of all, he came from a different social background and could boast of an Honourable in his family. I felt this more keenly than the other inadequacies, largely because a higher social status would have added piquancy to the aesthetic decadence for which we strove. I suppose that I was aiming at something between Oscar Wilde and Jimmy Porter. However, I realized that I did have one asset – Uncle Hector. Although he was not an aristocrat, he certainly looked like one, was colourful, very eccentric and lived in a unusual house.

It was at this time that I began to develop my repertoire of Uncle Hector stories. Raymond Foster was undeniably impressed, though he clearly considered I was overdoing it when I recounted a modified version of the night of the man-trap. He was totally uninterested in Darkie Hurrell, whose influence, as I maintained, had very nearly resulted in my taking zoology as my major subject in the sixth form instead of history. In retrospect, I can see that, in many ways, Foster was as well developed in his sarcastic critical faculties as the dreadful De Freville.

My representations of Uncle Hector and his exploits were so colourful that Raymond expressed a strong desire to meet him, partly, I think, because he suspected that I was making it up. Here he placed me in a very difficult position, because our relations with the owner of Ashbourne House were tenuous. He visited us only very occasionally, carefully timing his calls to avoid my father, and we now never went to Ashbourne.

Foster was so insistent in his desire to meet Uncle Hector that I eventually agreed, in a suitably casual manner, to take him to Ashbourne House. I realized that it would be unwise to mention this to my father and planned to engineer Raymond's visit as part of a cycle ride along that edge of the Downs. We left soon after luncheon on a golden, later October day.

I felt considerable trepidation as we puffed along the country lanes and downright fear when we alighted from our cycles outside the tall stone wall at Ashbourne House. I noticed that Uncle's hurdle contraption was no longer perched on the wall. It was when I was opening the carved door that I became aware of the marked difference between my clothes and Raymond's. He was in his young farmer's outfit and had had his hair cut. I, on the other hand, was still in my Wiltshire version of the costume of Montmartre, long hair, green shirt, red tie, dirty sandals and all.

With racing pulse I preceded Raymond along the brick path and knocked at the familiar front door. As we stood waiting for an answer, I gazed at the untidy elder hedge and remembered the two miserable dogs and their dreadful beatings.

There was the rattling of a chain. The door swung back

to reveal Uncle Hector in shirt sleeves and corduroy trousers. At first he did not recognize me – he had not seen me since I had entered my artistic phase. For a moment I thought he would throw us both out. But he gruffly invited us in and I nervously followed Raymond into the parlour, secretly wishing that we had been taken to the infinitely more impressive library. Raymond was clearly enjoying himself. He was relaxed and courteous as he removed his white riding mac.

'Wonderful old place you've got here, sir,' Foster commented in brisk tones, more appropriate to a second lieutenant in a Guards regiment than to a devoted admirer of Hans Arp. 'Our place is early Georgian, but I think that there is really nothing more appropriate for an English gentleman than a Tudor house,' he continued.

My uncle broke off a distinctly hostile examination of me and regarded my companion with a look of favour and growing interest. He grunted almost amiably and left the room. We heard him ordering Bunce to produce some tea and toast.

'I gather that you are a most distinguished archaeologist and historian,' the despicable Foster continued when my uncle returned.

That did the trick. In no time at all Raymond had Uncle Hector in his power. The old boy blossomed beneath his flattery. Even Miss Bunce was brought into the proceedings. What was more extraordinary, Uncle Hector looked quite kindly at Miss Bunce and asked her to bring in some lardy cake with the tea and toast.

Raymond was given a conducted tour of the house and then escorted round the estate while I sat in the kitchen with Miss Bunce, who was looking frail and snuffling from a newly acquired cold. I noticed that she now wore round, horn-rimmed spectacles. She seemed nervous and ill-at-ease and was obviously relieved to hear the booming of Uncle Hector's voice as he returned with Raymond through the door from the courtyard.

Uncle Hector walked with us to the front entrance. As we mounted our bicycles he turned to Raymond.

'I'll let you know when we'll be going.' He hesitated, glared at me, and then addressed Raymond again. 'Thorpe will be coming as well. We should have quite an interesting time.'

With that he shut the door and we started our eight-mile ride home as the evening mists crept across the Ashbourne watercress beds.

Raymond claimed to be greatly entertained by the visit. My uncle reminded him of a portrait by Erich Heckel. He was an 'absolute scream' and Raymond was greatly looking forward to meeting this Sid Thorpe character who was to accompany him and Uncle Hector to see an archaeological dig somewhere near Marlborough.

I was very cast down by what I regarded as Raymond's treachery to our artistic and intellectual values. But he laughed it off.

'All part of life's rich panorama,' he shouted as we whizzed down a steep lane between tall hazel hedges.

16

Raymond Foster's strange alliance with Uncle Hector was short-lived. It came to an abrupt end soon after their visit to the archaeological site near Marlborough. My uncle was so taken by Raymond's portrayal of the decent, clean-living young Englishman on that occasion that he had invited him to spend a day at Ashbourne House, with Sid Thorpe, to help sort out some of the relics. And that is when Raymond blotted his copybook.

Despite his sceptical dismissal of my story of the man-trap, Raymond was, nevertheless, tactless enough to raise the subject during his return visit to Ashbourne House. Looking back, it could have been a deliberate experiment or just pure devilment. Foster was so like De Freville in many ways.

According to his own account, Raymond began with an apparently innocent question. Did my uncle have a man-trap in his collection? Uncle Hector ignored this.

Raymond bided his time and then asked again whether it was true that there was a man-trap at Ashbourne House. No answer.

My friend made a third attempt.

'I understand, sir, that you used to set a man-trap to catch poachers.'

This yielded a dramatic response. My uncle spun round, white-faced with fury.

'Did James tell you that?'

'No-o, sir,' Raymond lied, I am thankful to say.

Foster left soon after this. He told me that he definitely did *not* like the look on my uncle's face.

Raymond gave us a most entertaining account, in the Astoria Café, of his adventures at Ashbourne. Aubrey Mason, who never knew what he was talking about, said that it was like something out of Chekhov.

An unexpected development of Raymond Foster's brief liaison with Uncle Hector was a more lasting relationship with Sid Thorpe. Sid had evidently taken a great liking to Raymond. The two of them had walked back across the fields after Raymond's abrupt departure from Ashbourne House. Raymond said that the walk nearly killed him. Even so the sprightly Sid Thorpe had been most affable and, with Raymond puffing along at his side, had tried to excuse his old friend's inexplicable rudeness following Raymond's innocent enquiries about man-traps.

It was during this walk that Sid Thorpe told Raymond that he had joined the Imperial Yeomanry with Uncle Hector and that they had been in South Africa together. Raymond discovered that they had had some remarkable adventures in the Boer War.

I was surprised to hear this. Uncle Hector rarely spoke of that war and never of his part in it. It now appeared that he had been involved in a particularly bloody and humiliating defeat by the Boers – on Christmas Day. Raymond could not recall many of the names, for he found Sid's talk of kopjes, kaffirs, kraals and commandos difficult to follow. Nevertheless he remembered the name of the Boer commander, De Wet, and that the action took place at Tweefontein – Raymond made a few pathetic puns about the names.

It was about twenty years later that I again came across De Wet and Tweefontein. I was glancing through some old copies of the *Fortnightly Review*. My attention was caught by an article entitled: DE WET'S LAST SUCCESS.

It slowly dawned on me that this was an account of Uncle Hector's Christmas Day battle and from Raymond Foster's still clearly remembered account, and my own enquiries, I was able to reconstruct what had gone on in that obscure defeat of British arms.

In mid-December 1901 Uncle Hector was riding with the 11th Battalion of the Imperial Yeomanry, part of a mobile force, 'Firman's Column', in the Eastern Free States. The CO, Lieutenant-Colonel Firman, DSO, was, at that time, on well-earned leave in Cape Town and the column was under the command of an ineffectual infantry major.

The whole countryside was infested with Boers under the able control of the guerrilla leader 'General' De Wet. They were successfully harrying the British force, which, a few days before Christmas, was ordered to take up a defensive position on an isolated hill, or kopje, at Tweefontein. The column consisted of three squadrons of Yeomanry and infantry detachments from the West Kents, East Kents, East Yorkshire and 24th Middlesex Regiments – about five hundred men in all.

Tweefontein Kop rose precipitously from the surrounding countryside, but sloped gently away on the side which the British column approached. The Boers had posted among the boulders on the kopje some snipers who fired a few shots before being driven off by a Yeomanry troop, which included Uncle Hector.

The British camp was established a hundred yards or so from the eastern edge of the kopje. The artillery, two fifteen pounders, was placed on the summit, at its western side, guarded by a handful of sentries.

According to Sid Thorpe, they were a very disgruntled

lot that camped in the shadow of Tweefontein Kop on the Christmas Eve of 1901. There were open disagreements between the officers, the usual scouting and foraging parties had not been sent out and they had nothing with which to celebrate the festive season.

At two o'clock on Christmas morning they were rudely awakened by a fusillade directed at their tents from the top of the kopje. Men were shot down as they scrambled from their tents or died from the bullets which ripped through the canvas. The adjutant was hit in the stomach, a major was riddled with shots, all the sergeants of the 34th, but one, died from bullet wounds in the head.

The devastating fire from rifles and Maxim guns continued for more than an hour. Uncle Hector and Sid Thorpe with a handful of other troopers sought cover behind an ambulance waggon, attempting to return the withering fire from the heights towering above them in the gloom of the African night.

Fifty-eight of my uncle's comrades were killed, eighty-four were wounded, two hundred and fifty were made prisoners on that terrible Christmas morning when the Boers crept up the steep western slopes of Tweefontein Kop to destroy Firman's Column.

Uncle Hector and Sid Thorpe were among the eight who escaped from the débâcle. Both were bleeding from hastily bandaged wounds: my uncle at the side of the head and Sid Thorpe on the left shoulder. They managed to find two horses and were away even before the Boers retired. They headed first for the native kraal at the base of the Kop and then turned towards the ruined Tweefontein farmhouse that they had seen from their encampment. Finding no possibility of shelter they continued across the dark veldt. They had intended making for the farm at Mooimeisjesrust, only two miles to the north-east (where General Sir Leslie Rundle was camped on a small hill, with two hundred and seventy Grenadier Guards) but were forced to gallop off to the west when they heard several parties of mounted Boers ahead of them. They rode towards a line of low hills and then through them on to open plain.

Just before dawn they spotted two horses tethered near some large scattered boulders. As they drew closer two kaffirs jumped up from behind the boulders and tried to mount the horses. According to Sid Thorpe, my uncle shouted at them to stop. They answered with a single rifle shot. Uncle Hector immediately fired back, killing one instantly with a shot through the head and wounding the other in the chest. Uncle Hector dismounted to search among the kaffirs' belongings for food and water. Sid Thorpe, who by now was feeling very weak, also dismounted and slumped on to the ground to rest. He said that he remembered my uncle opening a greasy cloth bundle, the kaffirs' sole belongings. He recalled my uncle grunting with surprise, as he took out some mealie cobs from the pathetic bundle and then, after re-tying the bundle, hanging it on his horse's saddle. My uncle handed Sid Thorpe a mealie cob, paused and then deliberately walked over to the wounded kaffir and shot him through the head. Sid explained that this was the humane thing to do with the 'poor devil'.

The two men rested until the sun was high in the sky and then cautiously turned back, to try again to join up with Rundle's Grenadiers. They eventually fell in with a squadron of Imperial Light Horse and were taken back to a field ambulance for treatment.

Sid Thorpe was as scarred by the memory of the rout at Tweefontein as my father had been by Passchendaele. Besides the shame of utter defeat, there was the gossip back in Johannesburg of incompetent cowardice and the false rumours that the men had been intoxicated from Christmas Eve celebrations.

It was a testimony to Raymond Foster's considerable, if insincere charm, that Sid Thorpe unburdened himself of such painful memories. Sid seemed not to have been unduly shocked by Uncle Hector's robbing and killing of the wounded kaffir, but the incident disturbed me greatly. It reminded me of my father's fever delirium which, as a child, I had believed was to do with his killing of German prisoners. It was also an unpleasant reminder that Uncle Hector was capable of what seemed to me to be cold-blooded murder and, again, revived childhood fears that I had been his guilty accomplice.

It seems that Sid Thorpe and Uncle Hector had been present at, and took considerable satisfaction in, vigorous counter-measures to clear the Boers from around Twee-fontein. Within weeks of humiliating defeat, they were part of the seven large columns, totalling sixty thousand troops, that swept through the countryside around Harrismith and which, by the following year, had crushed the resistance of De Wet's resourceful burghers.

Between us, Raymond and I managed to extract from Sid Thorpe the whole history of Uncle Hector's career in the Imperial Yeomanry during the years of the Boer War. We also discovered that Sid had subsequently spent some years 'roughing it' in Australia, before returning to Wiltshire to join the family business (straw and seed merchants) and that Uncle Hector had undertaken a sort of Edwardian Grand Tour including a few weeks' stay in Amsterdam, before coming home to buy Ashbourne House and settle down to the style of life with which I had been familiar since early childhood.

It seems not to have occurred to Sid Thorpe or to

Raymond to wonder how Uncle Hector had acquired the money to purchase Ashbourne House and to live a life unsullied by the need for productive employment. But I still remembered my parents' story that Uncle Hector had departed for South Africa with thirty pounds in his pocket and had returned, unaccountably, a relatively wealthy man. For some reason or other, I did not tell Raymond this. I suppose that my nose had been so put out of joint by his successes in finding out so much about my strange relative that I wanted to retain at least one secret.

I once tried probing Sid Thorpe on the matter when I found him by himself in our parlour, waiting for my father, who was upstairs sprucing himself up in preparation for one of their evening jaunts. I was very tactful, first mentioning how nice Ashbourne House must be looking at that time of the year, then speculating on the great cost of such a property at current prices and, finally, wondering how Uncle Hector could have afforded to buy such a wonderful place after coming straight out of the army as a trooper. It was quite easy, Sid explained: Uncle Hector's parents, despite their modest business, must have been better off than everyone supposed and had left him a tidy fortune. It often happened, he said. Sid recalled that when he returned from Australia his friend was already installed at Ashbourne, and that Uncle Hector's mother and father had died some time during or after the Boer War.

On the face of it Sid Thorpe's explanation was plausible, but I was still unconvinced. Looking back, I can see that I was quite right to be so, for two reasons. First, because I now recall that it was Uncle Hector's younger brother, Hert (the one killed on the Somme), who had told my mother that he had no idea how his brother had acquired his money. Secondly, there was the fact that Uncle Hector's mother had died *after* he had bought Ashbourne House. After all, hadn't my father always stressed, when enumerating his shortcomings, the fact that Uncle Hector had neglected his poor old mother while living in great splendour and complete idleness at Ashbourne?

17

In 1947, I reached the second stage of my long climb to academic obscurity – by gaining a university scholarship and a two-and-a-half inch spread in the the middle pages of the *North Wilts Herald and Advertiser*. Everyone seemed totally unprepared for my success. The headmaster clearly thought that there had been a serious administrative error; even my loyal mother was mildly surprised; Raymond Foster was furious. He had not gained an award, had failed outright in Greek and his irate father was making some very cutting remarks about Raymond's 'arty crafty' ways and his 'peculiar' friends. Raymond was forced to wear his young farmer's outfit almost continuously. Uncle Hector was outraged when he heard of my success and told my mother that universities were hotbeds of 'socialists, scroungers and army dodgers'.

Unfortunately, I was unable to join the 'army dodgers'. Instead I was abruptly translated into the Royal Army Medical Corps one terrible September day and languished for two bleak years at Aldershot as recruit, private, lance-corporal and finally, and very improbably, as a sergeant drill-instructor. Even this metamorphosis, which abruptly ended my artistic-intellectual pretensions, failed to meet with Uncle Hector's approval. On the only occasion he encountered me in uniform he spoke with heavy sarcasm of my joining the ranks of the 'Aspirin Boys', whom he regarded as little better than uniformed conscientious objectors.

As it turned out, that was the last time I spoke to Uncle Hector, for when I left the army and went up to university, I visited home only irregularly and then spent as much time as I could with my mother and father who, having survived my obnoxious adolescence, were now entirely congenial company.

My childish vision of university life was fulfilled as I progressed in easy stages from an undergraduate, to post-graduate research on Tudor land tenure and then to a Research Fellowship in my College.

It was in the year of my marriage to Molly, when I was still a Research Fellow, that death destroyed the frail human links with my childhood. My father unexpectedly expired from a heart attack early in 1955, and my mother followed four months later with leukaemia. Her final relapse was sudden and I was not at her bedside when she died. I have always felt remorse about this, because I had selfishly left early to return to College for the Founder's Day Feast. Mercifully Florrie was with her at the end, and told me that she spoke of my childhood days and, strangely, of the orchard at Ashbourne.

Uncle Hector did not come into the church for my mother's funeral, but I saw his tall figure standing beside the dark graveyard yews close to where I used to dump the discarded flowers when, as a child, I helped my mother tend to our family graves.

In the autumn of that year Uncle Hector also died. He was, I suppose, about eighty years old. Florrie telephoned to tell me of his death and two days later I drove down to Ashbourne for the funeral. There were only six other mourners: Miss Bunce in tears, Sid Thorpe, Thursa Titcombe and three elderly village women who, according to Thursa, came from mere nosiness. Miss Bunce did not

147

invite the mourners to the house, so I drove Sid Thorpe back to his home. He seemed greatly aged.

I was surprised to find, in view of our tortured relationship, that I felt a great loneliness and a deep sense of loss after Uncle Hector's funeral. His death was a break with so many distant memories. Yet, absurdly, I still did not understand how much he had shaped my life. It was not just my childish fears about the man-trap – these were deeply buried, as was my guilt over the betrayal of Darkie. I did not even recognize the other trap that my appalling, fascinating uncle had unwittingly set and which led to what I have now become – the helpless prey of the awful De Freville. My only protection at the time was a growing cynicism at life in general; my only escape – and how I wished I had followed it – the absorbing passion for wild creatures bequeathed by Darkie Hurrell.

It had not occurred to me to wonder about such a mundane matter as Uncle Hector's will. It was Molly who reminded me that I was his closest kin. The following week I received a letter from his solicitor informing me that I had been mentioned as a possible beneficiary in some of the fourteen versions of his will, one of which had been discovered in an old sock stuffed inside a grandfather clock.

Some weeks elapsed before I heard from Sid Thorpe, and then from the solicitor, that the last signed copy in the collection of wills named Miss Bunce as sole beneficiary. I must confess to a feeling of disappointment, for even though it seemed totally improbable that I would become the owner of Ashbourne House, I had, nevertheless, indulged in fantasies in which I invited the more congenial Fellows of my College for weekends at my Tudor house in Wiltshire.

It was still feeling disgruntled when a letter came from

Miss Bunce. It was written in a shaky, spidery hand with green ink on pale blue Basildon Bond writing paper and asked me to visit Ashbourne House. I received the cryptic invitation with very mixed feelings – notably wounded pride, frustrated avarice, curiosity, disappointment, embarrassment and nostalgia.

After a decent interval of a couple of weeks, I drove down to Ashbourne with Molly for the meeting with Bunce. I suppose that I still had some modest expectations; perhaps I would be given a choice of some of the more valuable of Uncle Hector's antiques. As I was soon to discover, Miss Bunce had no such intentions.

The old house looked shabby and forlorn as we walked up the familiar path now interlaced with weeds between the damp bricks. Miss Bunce took us into the parlour, warm and cosy in the otherwise cold and neglected house. We had tea with thin brown bread and honey, as we had the first time I stayed at Ashbourne House with Sandy, my grandfather, mother and father.

I was so overpowered with nostalgia that I found it impossible to converse and left it to Molly to chat to Miss Bunce about the difficulties of running such a large house single-handed. I remember that I was gazing at a decaying pink rose at the edge of the leaded window when I became conscious that Miss Bunce was speaking to me in a low shaky voice.

'Your uncle said that I was to talk to you about the will . . .' She paused and poked the glowing embers in the Queen Anne fire basket.

'About three months ago he told me that he intended leaving me the estate. I didn't know at the time that he had made so many wills.'

I nodded miserably as she continued.

'As you know, some of them left it all to you. I think it

was his devilment. It's funny. He seemed to resent you even as a boy.'

I nodded again, close to tears at the futility of it all.

'Your uncle wanted you to know that this house, and all the stuff in it, was not bought with family money. That went to his brother Hert when his mother died, although it was precious little, your uncle said.'

'Yes, I knew that,' I croaked. 'My mother told me.'

'Hert left his money to your mother during the First War after he was killed – on the Somme, I think it was. You knew that they were engaged?'

I shook my head. I hadn't known that.

'Your Uncle Hector brought money back from South Africa after the war there.'

I nodded.

'He told me about it three months ago. It was funny really because he never spoke about the Boer War and I never knew what he did in South Africa.'

Bunce poked the fire. I waited for her to continue.

'It was like a story. He said it happened on Christmas Day after a terrible battle in which his regiment was badly cut up. But he said that it was "the best damn Christmas Day" he ever had.'

'Tweefontein,' I ventured.

'Yes, that's the place,' Bunce continued. 'Apparently your uncle was lucky to escape from the Boers.'

Miss Bunce paused and shot me a sharp look.

'How did you know it was at Twee . . . whatever it was? He said he never told anyone else about it.'

'I'm a historian, I know about these things.'

'Well, anyway, your uncle got safely away from the Boers early on Christmas morning. 1901 I think he said it was.'

'Yes, that's right, Firman's Column and the Imperial

Yeomanry were cut up on Christmas Day 1901. Harold Parsons wrote about it.'

'Parsons? Did he come from around here?'

'No, he's a writer.'

'Ah well, what happened was that your Uncle Hector came across this wounded black man, all by himself out on this plain, early on Christmas morning. He gave your uncle an old bundle with some food in it. I suppose he realized that he was going to die and just gave it to your uncle. Seems like a miracle on Christmas Day and all.'

I agreed.

'God can work in very mysterious ways,' Miss Bunce mused piously. 'Because in that bag were some enormous uncut diamonds, all mixed up with corn cobs, your uncle said.'

So my father had not been so very wrong when he had muttered on about 'illegal diamond buying'. And the Kimberley diamond mines were only three days' ride from Harrismith.

'Well, I'm damned,' I ventured. My father's favourite ejaculation seemed the only entirely appropriate one under the circumstances. Curiously, it brought me great comfort.

'Did Uncle Hector say anything about Sid Thorpe on that Christmas morning?' I asked, as calmly as I could.

'No, he didn't. Of course he was in the army with Mr Thorpe, but he didn't say that he was with him when the old black gave him the bag with the corn cobs and the diamonds in it.'

Poor old Sid, little did he know what he was missing when he had slumped on to the ground while my uncle was examining the contents of the kaffir's bundle. The old bastard. That was why he had gone to Amsterdam

151

after the war, to flog the diamonds. He could keep his damned house, or at least Bunce could.

'Well, I have heard a few things in my time,' said Molly as we drove home. 'But that really takes some believing.'

'Yes, it does sound a bit like something out of Rider Haggard,' I answered.

I really didn't want to talk about it, not even to Molly, for I was remembering other things from the dim distance of my childhood: my father's row with Uncle Hector, Darkie Hurrell, the man-trap in the orchard and my mother's empty bed.

18

The visit to Miss Bunce with Molly, then so young and pretty, was the last time that I saw Ashbourne House. Within a year Miss Bunce had sold the house and land to a 'spec' builder and departed for Canada to live close to her sister. The old house was demolished, despite some local efforts to preserve it. Within another year, the orchard and fields, the mushroom barn, the outbuildings, the paddock, and the elder hedge were no more than memories. My uncle's little kingdom was now another kind of estate where two generations of children have played on neat lawns and countless cars have been polished on Sunday mornings. Only the pond remains, the scene of my uncle's act of piracy on my clockwork liner, a 'desirable feature' of the most pretentious bungalow with its picture window and patio where barbecues are held on summer evenings.

These were the most bitter moments of recall as I lay in the half-light at Molly's side. I had detected the source of the fresh-paint smell: a multi-coloured canvas was propped up on the dressing table. Yet when I closed my eyes, I saw two tiny skulls bathed in the reddish light of the dying sun and felt again the familiar tug of fear, hardly diminished after nearly fifty years. I slid into troubled sleep and dreamt of concealed metal teeth, two white sticks and a dark body lying in wet grass.

I awoke quite soon and crept down to the kitchen to read again the words marked by Florrie's pencilled lines.

ASHBOURNE RELICS PUZZLE EXPERTS

Building operations at the Downland Drive Estate at Ashbourne have revealed an enigma which puzzled archaeological experts called in from Trowbridge and Oxford.

The discovery was made on a building plot which had, until recently, formed part of the garden of 'Ridgeway View', No. 14 White Horse Crescent, Ashbourne, the home, for twenty-seven years, of Mr Arthur Marchant, a retired quantity surveyor, and his wife, Mrs Dorothy Marchant. Mr Marchant told our reporter that he intended selling part of his large and well-kept garden as a separate building plot. Mr Marchant explained that he had found it difficult at his age (69), to keep up such a large garden and, therefore had decided to split off a plot suitable for a bungalow to be built on. Unfortunately, this part of Mr Marchant's garden contained a pond on the only spot where a bungalow could be built and Mr Marchant decided to have it drained.

It was while Mr Marchant's pond was being drained that the discoveries were made, in the mud at the bottom of the pond. Workmen first came across a number of carved stone blocks. These were later identified as being of Roman origin. Beneath the stones was a skeleton. On one wrist was a Roman bronze torque, or bracelet. Near the skeleton was a Roman brooch, also made of bronze.

The skeleton was that of a six-foot male, between 40 and 60 years. The curious thing, and this is what puzzles the experts, is that it is almost less than a century old and may date from no more than 50 years ago.

The experts identified the bronze brooch as being of the 'Langton Down' type, which has a distinctive reeded bow. One of the stone blocks is an important find. It is an altar, some two feet high, dedicated to the goddess Diana. Her figure can be made out on the front of the altar stone, wearing a short tunic, carrying a bow and with a dog at her feet. The altar might have been intended to be portable and could have been used in a temporary shrine, but how it came to be in Mr Marchant's pond with the other carved stones is another mystery which the experts were unable to explain.

I refolded the newspaper and thrust it into my dressing gown pocket as pale morning light filtered through the kitchen window. So I had been right. My nightmares were quite true. I filled the electric kettle. The *North Wilts Herald and Advertiser* had told me plainly that my dotty uncle was a murderer and that I must share his guilt. I had warned Darkie about the sticks in the orchard, and then gone and fiddled with the damned things. Poor old Darkie. It was absurdly appropriate that he should have been buried beneath the altar of the goddess of the hunt.

I ate breakfast by myself and took Molly's up to her on a tray. I could not face the prospect of a further post-mortem on her latest picture – not on that morning.

It was misty, with weak sunlight barely filtering through lowering clouds, as I drove into College. The car-park was empty and Len, the oldest of the College porters, was intent on gossip. It took all the skill I had developed over nearly thirty years to get away from him. As I walked across the quad De Freville bore down on me, waving a fistful of pages.

'Dr Yeo. Dr Yeo! I have tried to redraft the essay, but with the best will in the world I can find precious little, or not to put too fine a point on it, *no* evidence for the influence of the Black Death . . . '

'Piss off, De Freville,' I growled.

It was disgraceful, and I would no doubt hear about it from the Senior Tutor, but I was evidently an accomplice in murder – so what had I to lose?

I had been badly shaken by that piece in the paper. For years I had convinced myself that my fears about a man-trap and a murder had been merely childish imaginings. I never saw the man-trap in the grass and it had all seemed so improbable. But I had been right all those

155

years ago – except that I hadn't worked out where the body had been hidden.

I had reached my College room and was fiddling with the keys, when it dawned on me that there was no mention in the newspaper article of any damage to the skeleton. The trap would have been unlikely to have broken any leg bones, but if, as I had always imagined, Uncle Hector had clubbed the poor devil to death then surely the skull would have been fractured or some other bones broken?

Could Uncle Hector have been so deranged as to have stood over the body of a trapped human being and savagely beaten him to death? In 1935 (as I remember Darkie saying)? He beat the poor dogs at Ashbourne and he beat the other poacher, and as I discovered, was capable of shooting and robbing a kaffir near Tweefontein.

I knelt down to light the gas fire that had hissed away and warmed me for nearly thirty years, trying to avoid the most painful question of all. As the ancient device thudded into life, the vision of an empty torchlit bed forced itself into my mind. I could see again the depression that my mother's body had left in the feather mattress and remembered her lingering scent. What on earth was she doing that night? How did the brooch that Darkie gave to her find its way into his grave?

I scrambled to get up and then slumped down again, staring into the glowing heat until my eyes hurt. She seemed to have aged from that time. Whatever had happened must have been so very terrible for her.

I was aroused by a knock at the door, croaked out a command to 'wait', pulled myself to my feet and opened the door to face the garrulous Len, bearing my mail, still bent on gossip. I stood limply in the draughty doorway as the old man gave his views on female undergraduates and the damage done at the Boat Club Dinner on the previous night.

After Len departed, I recovered enough to lift one of the unmarked essays from the pile on my desk. I read three quite briskly, even managing a sarcastic comment in the margin of the second, before seizing up completely. I fished out the now crumpled copy of the *North Wilts Herald and Advertiser* from my pocket. I wished aloud that Florrie had not sent the thing. It was at that moment that I recalled what Florrie had told me, all those years before, about my mother's dying memories, when, of all things, she had spoken about the orchard at Ashbourne. Florrie had said my mother's words had not made any sense to her – perhaps they held some clues for me.

I found Florrie's telephone number in my diary. I always copied it in each year, so that I could phone her on Christmas Day. I dialled and waited, flicking over the pages of essay number four. Then I heard the familiar, now frail, Wiltshire voice.

'Yes?'

'Hello, Florrie. It's James Yeo here.'

'Who is that?'

'It's James. James Yeo.'

'Oh, Master James. How nice. Where are you? Why are you ringing? You usually telephone on Christmas Day.'

'Yes, I know, but I wanted to ask you something . . . about my mother.'

'About Mrs Yeo?'

'Well, it's about what she said to you at the end. You were with her when she . . . passed on.'

'Yes, I was. You had to go back on some important business – if you remember.'

'That's right. But I wondered if you could recall what she said about the orchard at Ashbourne House. I think you said that it did not make any sense.'

There was no answer.

'Florrie. Are you there?'

'I'm still here, Master James.'

'Well, what did Mother say to you . . . at the end . . . that didn't make any sense to you?'

'It *did* make sense – all of it.'

'Then why did you say it didn't?'

'Because I promised your mother – years before – that I wouldn't.'

'What do you mean, "years before"?'

Florrie ignored my question.

'Are you ringing me because of what you read in the newspaper that I sent you this week?'

'Yes. Yes. That's exactly why I'm ringing.'

'I thought so. I didn't know whether to mark that bit about the things they have dug up at Ashbourne, but I thought that it would look odd if I didn't. I didn't think that you would know anything about what went on there.'

'Florrie, what are you talking about? And what did you mean about promising my mother "years before"?'

'It was when she came back from Ashbourne. You remember she went to look after your Uncle Hector when he had pneumonia and Miss Bunce was in Canada?'

I'll say I did. I waited for Florrie to continue.

'Well, she was very upset when she came back. She broke down once, when we were alone together. I was frightened, I can tell you. It was then that she told me.'

'Told you *what*, Florrie?' I yelled into the telephone, upsetting the pile of examination papers on to the carpet.

'Told me about the man that was caught in the man-trap in your Uncle Hector's orchard.' Florrie contrived to

158

sound matter-of-fact while carefully emphasizing each syllable.

'Mother told you . . . ?'

'Yes. She told me that Uncle Hector and Miss Bunce had heard the poor man shouting in the orchard.'

'Miss Bunce?' I had forgotten that she had returned on the afternoon of that terrible day.

'Miss Bunce and your uncle were . . . well, like man and wife, so they were . . . well, like together, when it happened.'

Like together? Miss Bunce and Uncle Hector? How disgusting. He always treated her like a slave.

'Yes,' Florrie continued. 'Your uncle was . . . '

There was a long pause.

'You'll have to excuse me, Master James, but I've got something in the oven and milk will be boiling over if I don't get on . . . I can't tell you any more. I've got to get on . . . '

'Florrie,' I squeaked. 'Florrie, don't ring off. I'll wait. Please . . . '

I pleaded with her as I used to as a child when I wanted something badly. There was crackling telephonic silence. I was exploding with impatience.

After what seemed an eternity, I heard scraping and bumping noises. I waited expectantly, only to hear a click and the purring dialling tone.

I redialled, my hands shaking with frustrated excitement and rage. Blast Florrie. I was almost glad that I had locked her in the larder that distant morning. I kicked at the untidy pile of examination papers on the carpet.

There was no reply. I dialled repeatedly – there was never an answer.

I was trying for the sixth time when there was a double knock on the door. I made no answer. Then there was a single tap, the handle turned and the door slowly opened to reveal De Freville's head.

'You must excuse me, Dr Yeo, but in view of what happened earlier this morning I feel constrained . . .' He hesitated and stepped into the room. 'Are you all right . . . sir?'

'What do you want, De Freville?'

'Well, I feel, under the circumstances, that . . . in view of the . . . eh . . . Black Death – are you sure you're all right, sir?'

'Perfectly, De Freville,' I lied.

I advanced menacingly; De Frevilled retreated behind the door. Only his head was showing. He gulped, opened his mouth, closed it and then abruptly withdrew. I closed the door and sat down to commune once more with my ancient heater.

I spent the rest of the morning fidgeting, tidying up the scattered essay papers, making two cups of instant coffee and gazing out of my window. What was Florrie doing? If she was worried about the milk boiling over and had something in the oven, she would be unlikely to be going out. Why had she put the telephone back when she knew that I was waiting? It had to be something to do with my mother. Florrie knew what had gone on in that godforsaken orchard and was frightened to tell me about it. If I had only kept my fingers off that stick, none of this would have happened.

By midday I had calmed down sufficiently to creep over to the dining hall for an early lunch, then hid behind *The Times* with a black coffee in the Combination Room before retreating. I resisted the temptation to telephone Florrie yet again. She would know it was me. Better to wait. She might think that I had given up, then I could get through to her in the evening and talk her round. I used to be able to wheedle most things out of Florrie.

19

I left College early that evening. It was mild and damp. The street lamps shed yellow cones of light in gathering mist.

I reached home just after six. Molly was clattering about in the kitchen to the sound of the News on Radio 4. I made straight for the telephone in my room.

Once more I dialled Florrie's number and waited, watching the jerky progress of the second-hand on the desk clock. After twelve seconds the ringing tones were checked by an abrupt click.

'Is that you, Florrie? This is James here again. We were cut off this morning.'

I waited for the familiar voice of my childhood. 'Florrie?'

There was no reply, only the resumption of the dialling tone. Damn it. She had hung up again. It was too bad of her. Mother wouldn't have stood such nonsense. Once she had made Florrie take her shoes off in the search for a ten shilling note that I had purloined from the back of the china cupboard to buy some Muggsy Spanier records. It dawned on me that Florrie must have known who had taken the money.

The door opened and Molly appeared, flushed from her culinary exertions, carrying a cup of tea. I was slumped dismally in the chair. I realized that some explanation was necessary.

'I've tried to phone Florrie all day. She's just hung up on me. I can't understand what's the matter with her.'

'Why on earth are you ringing *her*? And in such a state. You forgot to telephone her last Christmas. I kept reminding you, all day, and you never did.'

'Well, I was busy – you may remember . . . Oh hell, it doesn't matter.'

It was then that I began to tell Molly what had happened. This time it didn't sound at all improbable – as it had when I blurted it out to Fatty Higgins and to Bowen all those years ago. Molly nodded.

'So that's what it's all about. I always knew you had some fixation about your Uncle Hector and a man-trap.'

'How could you? I've never told you about . . .'

'Yes you did, years ago. Not long after we were married. You told me about a man-trap with someone caught in it by your Uncle Hector at Ashbourne, I suppose, before the war.'

'I never . . .'

'Yes, when you had a cyst on your tummy, and convinced yourself that you were going to die of cancer. You told me quite a lot of interesting things then, as a matter of fact.'

Molly continued remorselessly.

'And, what is more, you also went on about murder, man-traps and God alone knows what else when you had your tooth out.'

'Ah . . . ' I ventured.

'Yes, you did. You were so scared of the needle that you insisted on a general anaesthetic and then broke the chair, by trying to stand up in it, as soon as the dentist tried to put the clip in your mouth. Your mother said that your Uncle Hector once did *exactly* the same thing. He laid out the dentist – woke up to find him unconscious in the corner of the surgery.'

'Yes, but . . . '

162

'And when you were breaking the chair you were shouting at the top of your voice about man-traps and bloody murder. Mr Witherspoon told me about it.'

Molly paused and took a sip from what I imagined was to have been my cup of tea just as the telephone rang. I gesticulated to her to take the call.

'It could be Florrie,' I hissed. 'She may have changed her mind. She might talk to you.'

'Of course she won't ring, James. She won't have changed her mind in a few minutes.'

'Well, just answer – please.'

Molly was right, it was not Florrie. I listened, with increasing gloom, to what was evidently turning into a friendly conversation with the Senior Tutor. I made a frog face and shook my head.

Molly regarded me with her amused, detached look and continued to tell the Senior Tutor of the wonders of her latest oil paintings. The conversation finished with several alternating yeses and noes from Molly and the assertion that I had not yet arrived home.

'The Senior Tutor wants to speak to you about an undergraduate called De Freville. He says would you ring back when you get in.'

I knew what that would be about. I thought of the Senior Tutor nodding sympathetically while De Freville recounted the enormities to which he had been subjected. I had no intention of telephoning the Senior Tutor that night or the next one if it came to that. I was going down to find Florrie and wring the truth out of her.

I became conscious that Molly was rattling on again.

' . . . so if we leave early we can be in Wiltshire before lunch . . .'

'Eh?'

'We can be in Wiltshire before lunch. Then we can

163

corner Florrie and sort the whole thing out,' Molly continued briskly. 'It's obvious that I shan't get any sense out of you until we do. I shall be quite intrigued to find out myself and I can make a few sketches of the Downs for a picture I want to do. You've no Saturday morning lectures this term, so there's no reason why we shouldn't go.'

I quite enjoyed being bossed about that evening, especially on an issue about which I had already decided. Molly was very like my mother in many ways. I could see that if anyone was going to get something out of Florrie it would be Molly, by, I suspected, basically the same techniques as Mother would have used. Poor old Florrie. I supposed that she was suffering severe pangs of conscience at having unthinkingly betrayed Mother's confidences – or was there some other reason?

It was a clear morning, with pale sunshine dispersing the last traces of mist from ploughed fields and hedgerows, as we drove in the Marina along straight empty roads. We had coffee at Buckingham.

It was while we were driving through a narrow street at one end of the small town that I asked Molly why she had never taxed me about the man-trap (and Uncle Hector) if she had known about them for so long.

She found it difficult to answer my question.

'I don't know, really. It was very improbable. You must admit that. There was no way that I could put two and two together. Perhaps, underneath, I was frightened at what it might mean. I don't know.'

It was about half past eleven when we drove up to Florrie's small, neat terraced house. We parked the car round the corner and walked back to a white-painted gate. A plump tabby cat sat cleaning itself on the sill of

164

the single downstairs window. As I opened the gate I noticed a sparkling empty milk bottle on the step of the green front door. In the window I could see, between the lace curtains, a plaster Alsatian dog and a potted plant.

I knocked three times. The sound echoed within. Intuitively, I felt that the house was empty. I knocked again. There was no reply. The cat jumped from the window sill and bolted underneath a small privet hedge.

It was while I was contemplating walking round to the back of the house that the door of Number 14 opened to reveal a plump elderly lady, who seemed to have forgotten to put in her false teeth.

'Did you want Miss Ayres?' she spluttered.

'Yes, do you know where she is?'

'She've gone over to her sister's at Cricklade. Went on the early bus, she did.'

'Damn – I'm sorry. You see we've driven a long way to see Miss Ayres.'

'Then why don't you drive to Cricklade to find her?' Florrie's neighbour suggested.

'You know where her sister lives?'

'Course I do. Been over there myself with Florrie a couple of times,' she announced importantly. 'Nice little place Florrie's sister's got. Quite near her daughter and the grandchildren. Got two she has – Kevin and Tracey. Her husband used to be on the roads . . .'

'Yes. Thank you. But could you tell us where she lives?'

'Oakington Road, Number 28. You can't miss it. It's on the first corner as you drive in.'

We shouted our thanks and within seconds were heading for Cricklade.

Number 28, Oakington Road turned out to be at the end of a row of semi-detached, pre-war council houses.

165

In the garden was an elderly black and brown dog of indeterminate breed. It walked stiffly towards us, barked perfunctorily and accompanied us to the front door. My knock soon produced the rattling of a chain and lock on the other side of the door. Then there was silence. Just as I was preparing to knock once more a small head peered round the corner of the house.

'What do you want?' A girl of about six years old came into full view.

'We want to find Miss Ayres . . . Florrie Ayres . . . Great-Aunt Florrie. We understood that she was here.'

The child shook her head solemnly.

'You mean she's *not* here?'

The child nodded.

'Then where is she?'

At that, Tracey (for I assumed it was she) disappeared. I was near exploding with frustration and, if Molly had not prevented me, would have battered further on the front door.

After a few moments the child reappeared.

'Grandma's on the lav,' she announced.

Molly's hand squeezed mine. I could feel her mirth. I opened my mouth just as Tracey resumed.

'Nana Florrie's gone to see someone round the corner – at that house over there.' She pointed across a field to a bungalow on the main road which we had passed on our search for Number 28, Oakington Road.

'Over there?'

As we retraced our steps to the car, I realized that Cricklade had again intruded into my life. It was not only the Wool Trade, 1536–1546. The mysterious altar stone that had been Darkie's hidden monument had come from Cricklade. I had the creepy feeling that I was part of some predetermined pattern. But why Cricklade *again* of all places?

Florrie's third refuge turned out to be a sort of mock-Tudor bungalow. It was built of imitation Cotswold stone and set back a hundred yards or so from the road behind a tall beech hedge. The path to the front door was lined by dark yew bushes. Six starlings were feeding and quarrelling at the edge of a circular flower bed in a neat lawn. Molly knocked twice on the large brass knocker, which seemed strangely familiar. After a few seconds I could see the indistinct outline of a tall woman through the oval of frosted glass in the green front door.

There was a sliding of a lock. The door opened to reveal Miss Bunce. She was wearing gold-rimmed glasses and looked hardly any older than when I had last seen her, nearly thirty years before. At that instant I remembered where I had seen the door knocker – at Ashbourne House.

Miss Bunce did not recognize me. I stood transfixed. Behind her in the small gloomy hall I could see Florrie, looking wizened and pale.

Molly glanced sharply at me and then spoke. I cannot remember what she said; I was still in a state of shock. Then Miss Bunce recognized me and stepped back into the hall.

'Come in, James. This *is* a surprise.' Her voice had the same quavering uncertainty that I remembered from so long ago.

In a daze I followed Molly into the bungalow. Miss Bunce motioned us into a room on the right. Florrie preceded us. I could see that she and Miss Bunce had been taking tea together.

'We were just passing through,' I explained. 'We were told that Florrie was here. I didn't know that you were

. . . ' I nearly said 'dead' and then seized up. My mouth was completely dry.

'Yes, we were looking for Florrie,' Molly continued lamely and then faltered into a silence. Florrie was standing behind a chintz-covered wing chair. She avoided my stare.

For the next ten minutes Miss Bunce related her history – how her widowed sister in Toronto had died and her nephew and niece had married and moved away. She had returned only that summer to Cricklade – her birthplace. It was a month since she had run into Florrie. Miss Bunce never mentioned Uncle Hector and only once referred to her life at Ashbourne House.

Molly then rattled on about our doings, declined the offer of tea and drew on her gloves.

'We've got to be getting on,' she announced briskly. 'Can we give you a lift, Florrie?'

To my surprise, for she had only to walk back to her sister's, Florrie accepted Molly's invitation. She preceded us to the front door and waited for Molly and me to take leave of Miss Bunce – which we did with insincere promises to call in next time we were in the district.

I glanced at my watch; it was only two o'clock. Miss Bunce's offer of tea had made the afternoon seem much later. I felt an urgent need for a stiff drink. I had noticed a pleasant-looking, stone-built pub on our journey into Cricklade and suggested that we drop in there. Florrie shook her head. She had to get back to her sister's, she said.

With some difficulty Molly persuaded Florrie to get into the car, for a 'nice chat' before we left. Florrie sat in the back. She looked tired and worried. I imagined Miss Bunce lurking, only a few feet away, behind the beech hedge.

'Now then Florrie,' I commenced. 'What *is* this all about?'

Florrie did not answer at once. She looked down and fiddled with her handbag before regarding me directly.

'You know very well what it's about, James.' It was the first time she had ever called me by my christian name alone.

'All right then – why did you ring off when I telephoned you?'

'Because I didn't want to break my word to your mother and I didn't want to get Miss Bunce into trouble.' Florrie looked at me accusingly. 'You were always a very persistent boy and you could be quite vindictive if you put your mind to it.' She paused and chose her words carefully. 'Like when you locked me in the larder for a whole morning. Or when you painted the dog.'

'Come on Florrie, they were only jokes.'

'Well, it didn't seem very funny to me.'

'Sandy quite liked being painted, I remember. It was washing it off that he didn't like.'

'And who was it that had to clean him?' Florrie retorted. It came as a shock: the realization that Florrie didn't like me.

'Florrie, what did you mean, "get Miss Bunce into trouble"?'

'Well, you might have made trouble. I always thought that you were very put out about not inheriting Ashbourne House when your Uncle Hector died.'

'Florrie, it's my mother I want to know about. Don't you remember the Roman brooch that Darkie gave her? It was with the other things in the pond at Ashbourne.'

'You surely don't think that your mother . . . '

'No, of course not . . . '

169

It was then that Molly interrupted. She was looking at me as she spoke.

'Now look Florrie. Don't you think it would be better if you let us know what Mrs Yeo told you? James has guessed most of it anyway and his Uncle Hector is dead and can't get you into any trouble.' Molly hesitated. 'The thought of him cudgelling someone like that is . . .'

'But it wasn't him, Florrie blurted out. 'It was Miss Bunce.'

Florrie lowered her voice to a whisper. I had to strain to hear her.

'You see, your uncle had a gun with him. When he and Miss Bunce got to the orchard he handed it to her, so that she could sort of cover the poacher while your uncle tried to release his leg from the trap.'

I could imagine poor Bunce, tall and droopy, snatched from a warm bed and the arms of her employer standing (in a nightdress?) with the gun wobbling in her hands.

'It was while your uncle was trying to release the poor man that Miss Bunce shot him.'

'Miss Bunce shot him?' Miss Bunce. It was unbelievable.

'Yes. You see the man hit out with a great stick at your uncle. Miss Bunce panicked and just fired right into his chest.' Florrie paused to clear her throat.

'It was then, James, that your mother came on the scene, for she had heard the shouting and the shot and saw the light moving in the orchard.'

'Is that exactly as she told you, Florrie?'

'Yes. I'm certain it is. Your mother stayed with the man who was still in the trap, while your uncle took Miss Bunce away.'

I pictured my mother crouching in the dark orchard tending Darkie as he lay dying in the long grass. Thank

God she did not know that I had been to the place before her that night.

Florrie droned on.

'By the time your uncle returned the man was dead. Your mother placed her brooch in his top pocket: I am sure she said it was the top pocket. You remember the Roman brooch that Darkie Hurrell gave her?'

It was only then that I realized that Florrie did not know who had been trapped.

'Florrie, don't you know who was caught in the trap?'

'No, it was just a poacher, I suppose.'

'It was *Darkie Hurrell*, Florrie.'

'Oh dear. Are you sure? Mrs Yeo never said that it was Darkie. I thought he did a flit a long time before.'

'Yes, he did a flit to Ashbourne. Don't you remember that he always wore the Roman bracelet, on his wrist. They found it on the skeleton in the pond.'

'Oh dear. You were so fond of Darkie. He gave you the jackdaw. I'm so sorry.' She gave me a long look.

'I had guessed it was him a long time ago.'

Florrie fortunately missed the significance of my reply and continued.

'Well, your mother went to look after Miss Bunce.' Florrie paused. 'And that's really about all your mother told me. I promised her that I would never tell. I should not have told you, but you seemed to have guessed it anyway and besides, it was all so long ago.'

We all sat in silence. The car windows were steaming up. Molly wound down her window. I watched Florrie as she took out a handkerchief from her handbag. She seemed so shrivelled and frail. Neither of them knew about the stick which I had shifted in the orchard on that distant summer night. I had not been able to bring myself to confess to Molly what I had done. Only Fatty Higgins

171

and Bowen had known and neither had believed me. I thought of Mrs Bowen diving in the river near here, her white limbs so perfect. She too would be old and wrinkled – or dead.

'Are you sure we can't drive you home, Florrie?' Molly wheedled. 'Perhaps we could have tea somewhere.'

Florrie shook her head and snapped shut her handbag.

'Florrie, why did you come to see Miss Bunce?' I asked.

'Because I was frightened about what you might do if you knew . . . I was going to warn her, but couldn't bring myself to say anything when I got there . . . she seemed different . . . we just talked about my sister.' Florrie paused and put her hand on the door handle.

'She's had quite a lot of trouble since her operation.'

With that, Florrie made her escape. The car rocked as she slammed the door shut with surprising vigour.

It was a final gesture. I leaned across to wave through Molly's open window and then started the car. Molly wound up the window as we drove slowly to the end of the road and halted, waiting for a break in the traffic to turn into the main road.

I looked in the car mirror and saw Florrie's tiny figure, blurred by the still misty back window. I looked away and glanced again in the mirror to see the indistinct, but unmistakable, figure of Miss Bunce standing with Florrie beside the tall beech hedge. They stood together for a few moments and then, I could tell from her posture, Miss Bunce propelled Florrie from view, back through the garden gate.

A warm autumnal sun shone on the Vale of the White Horse as we drove through flat meadowland towards the rising edge of the Downs. We parked the car in a muddy lane near a straggling wood of hawthorns, hazels and stunted oaks, crossed a wooden bridge over a weed-choked brook and followed a chalk track along a steep-sided coombe. There were a few scraggy thorns, a line of beeches and then the swelling grey-green of the open downland. Peewits were calling and tumbling in the clear air. We climbed up on the buoyant turf and perched on the lip of the chalk escarpment. Away to the north the Cotswolds were hidden in bluish mist.

Molly was sketching thistles and tall clouds and grassy slopes as I gazed idly at the sky. Then I grew restless and climbed higher for a distant view of Wayland's Cave. It was hidden in encircling beeches among line after line of downs that stretched away to the north-west. The solitude was pierced by a skylark's song. The spectre of Uncle Hector was already receding. I was not joined to him by the guilt of murder in the dark orchard. Most wonderful of all, my mother had tended Darkie and been with him at the end.

I ran down to Molly, jumping and leaping on the springy turf as I had done as a boy. We shared my bar of chocolate and sat together until the hills were tinged with apricot and gold. We started down in failing light as a faint curved moon appeared at the dying sunset's edge. Below us the beeches were silhouetted against darkening sky. It was then that I heard the eerie, shrill wailing all around us on the hillside. There must have been scores of them. Darkie's darlings – stone curlews. They were preparing to fly south.

The world's greatest novelists now available in Panther Books

Angus Wilson

Such Darling Dodos	£1.50	☐
Late Call	£1.95	☐
The Wrong Set	£1.95	☐
For Whom the Cloche Tolls	£1.25	☐
A Bit Off the Map	£1.50	☐
As If By Magic	£2.50	☐
Hemlock and After	£1.50	☐
No Laughing Matter	£1.95	☐
The Old Men at the Zoo	£1.95	☐
The Middle Age of Mrs Eliot	£1.95	☐
Setting the World on Fire	£1.95	☐
The Strange Ride of Rudyard Kipling (non-fiction)	£1.95	☐
Anglo-Saxon Attitudes	£2.95	☐

John Fowles

The Ebony Tower	£1.95	☐
The Collector	£1.95	☐
The French Lieutenant's Woman	£2.50	☐
The Magus	£2.50	☐
Daniel Martin	£2.95	☐
Mantissa	£1.95	☐
The Aristos (non-fiction)	£1.95	☐

Brian Moore

The Lonely Passion of Judith Hearne	£1.50	☐
I am Mary Dunne	£1.50	☐
Catholics	£1.50	☐
Fergus	£1.50	☐
The Temptation of Eileen Hughes	£1.50	☐
The Feast of Lupercal	£1.50	☐
Cold Heaven	£1.95	☐

To order direct from the publisher just tick the titles you want and fill in the order form.

All these books are available at your local bookshop or newsagent, or can be ordered direct from the publisher.

To order direct from the publisher just tick the titles you want and fill in the form below.

Name _____

Address _____

_____

Send to:
Panther Cash Sales
PO Box 11, Falmouth, Cornwall TR10 9EN.

Please enclose remittance to the value of the cover price plus:

UK 45p for the first book, 20p for the second book plus 14p per copy for each additional book ordered to a maximum charge of £1.63.

BFPO and Eire 45p for the first book, 20p for the second book plus 14p per copy for the next 7 books, thereafter 8p per book.

Overseas 75p for the first book and 21p for each additional book.